*Erotica 2:
Bettina and Candy*

also from Bettina Varese:

EROTICA 1: BETTINA'S TALES

Erotica 2:
Bettina and Candy

collected by
Bettina Varese

COLLECTIVE PUBLISHING

Copyright © THE COLLECTIVE PUBLISHING COMPANY

First published in 2000 by
THE COLLECTIVE PUBLISHING COMPANY

ISBN 0 9535290 1 0

All rights reserved. No part of this publication may be reproduced,
stored in a retrieval system, or transmitted, in any form or by any means
without the prior written permission of the publisher, nor be otherwise
circulated in any form of binding or cover other than that in which
it is published, and without a similar condition being
imposed on the subsequent purchaser.

All characters and all events are purely fictitious,
and any resemblance real or fancied to actual
persons or events is entirely coincidental.

Stories collected by Bettina Varese
Edited by Judy Keaton & Simon Starkwell
Designed and Typeset by The Collective Publishing Co

Printed and bound in Great Britain
by Cox and Wyman Ltd
Reading, Berkshire

COLLECTIVE PUBLISHING
P.O. Box 10, Sunbury on Thames, TW16 7YG, United Kingdom
www.collectivepublishing.com

COLLECTIVE PUBLISHING

ENGLAND

Bettina writes,

I always carry a condom wherever I go. Make sure you also practise safe sex.

Contents

TEACHER'S PETS
1

SISTERS IN SIN
25

BACK SEAT BITCHES
39

THE INTERVIEW
55

Contents

SPANKING
75

RIDING A JAGUAR
89

COMING CLEAN
107

THE ANGEL ROOM
125

Contents

RED OBSESSION
141

JUST PRESS PLAY
157

Dear Reader,

Welcome to my second collection of erotic stories. Thank you for all the letters you sent me saying how much you enjoyed my first book 'Erotica 1: Bettina's Tales'. I hope you like this one just as much. In this book I'm going to introduce you to a really good friend of mine, Candy. She has helped me put this collection together. Can you imagine two girls together in one room for days on end, reading through hundreds of sexy stories. I can tell you it got very hot in there, and we only had each other to relieve our sexual tension. It's a wonder that we got any work done at all! I'll be telling you more about Candy later on in the book, and she'll be introducing some of the stories. Just thinking about her is making my pussy wet, so I'll let you read on, while I . . . ooh yes!

Much love,
Bettina
xxx

Bettina writes,

I love the way this story begins, that's why I made it the first story in the book. 'Teacher's Pets' reminds me of when I was studying at University. There were always rumours flying around about relationships between students and lecturers. Mainly just in our imaginations of course. But there were a few girls who were prepared to do anything to get good grades. It was mainly petting and blow jobs because of the risk of pregnancy. I remember one girl in particular who was very popular with the male teachers. She wasn't very academic, but she had the most gorgeous full lips, and she was always touching up her lipstick. She left Uni with an honours degree!

I don't know if 'Teacher's Pets' is a true story but I like to believe it is. See what you think . . .

Teacher's Pets

TEACHER'S PETS

Mike leaned back languidly in his chair.

"Use your tongue!" he commanded. His eyes contemplated Monique's large, magnificent breasts, outlined through her stretch T-shirt. "Th-, th-," he demonstrated. "Thesis."

"Seesis," repeated Monique.

"No, no. Thesis. Try it at the end of the word: Teeth. Thesis."

"Teess. Teesis."

Mike sighed. Teasers, yes - that's what they were, all right. "Keep working at it," he said to Monique, making a swift mark on the sheet of paper in front of him. "Next . . . . Tania, would you read the next paragraph?"

Stumbling, Tania began to struggle with the text. Mike looked round the class. It was the height of summer, with the sun blazing in through the window, and there was a lot of nubile female flesh on view; bare sun-bronzed shoulders and midriffs, and plenty of cleavage bursting out of skimpy T-shirts. Not for him, though. How he resented being deprived of the perks which, in his younger days, had made teaching English to young foreign girls such a pleasurable experience. Looking at the students, he could see from the dark circles around their eyes, and their generally debauched air of physical exhaustion, that this lot had enjoyed as exuberant a night-life as any. No doubt, he thought bitterly, they had invited his younger colleague to share it with them - that obnoxious Bob, with his cocky laugh and his swaggering walk . . .

"Thank you, Tania," he said. "Next!"

Well, it was several years since he'd got in on the action. Not that there was supposed to be any action between staff and students - the rules strictly forbade male tutors from visiting any female's room unchaperoned, and occasionally there was a bit of a fuss. He'd never had any trouble though, the mademoiselles and the senoritas had always been happy enough to have him - then.

Mike was still brooding when, in his office after class, he began to fill in the final mark sheet. The course finished the next day, and they would all be going back home to their own countries. Perhaps it was time he gave up teaching on these courses. A few years ago he had counted on three weeks of unrestrained sexual pleasure; now it was three weeks of unrelieved sexual frustration. Their loss, he tried to console himself. They don't know what they're missing.

There was a knock at the door.

"Come in . . . Yes Monique?"

"Mister Eel," she began.

"Hill," Mike corrected automatically.

"Mister 'ill, I come to ask you about my mark."

"Your mark? I'm afraid I can't discuss your mark at this stage."

"You see, it is very important for me. My father, he will be very angry if I do not do well." She blinked at him coyly, moistening her top lip with the tip of her pink tongue.

Mike returned her gaze severely. The little baggage, he thought, she thinks she can get round me by flaunting her cleavage at me all morning, then coming here and fluttering her eyelashes.

"Your mark will reflect the progress you have made during these three weeks," he replied officiously. "Any student who is dissatisfied may ask to be reassessed by another tutor . ."

Monique was shaking her head. "No, no. I, er . ."

Clearly she was having difficulty expressing herself. For a moment a thought flickered across his mind . . how much did getting a good mark matter to her? But no, surely not that much . . . did it? He watched her carefully. If he made the first move she might scream rape and cause all sorts of trouble for him.

She had come right up to his desk now, standing so close that he could smell her musky perfume.

"I would do anything I could to improve my mark, Mister 'ill," she cooed softly. "Please . . . I fuck you?"

Mike was shocked at her blatant question. Not much doubt over her intentions now. His cock stiffened, straining against his trousers. He reached out his left hand and ran his fingers down her bare arm, feeling the soft warmth of her skin. She closed her eyes and parted her lips as if she had longed for his touch. Mike hoped that it was true, that she'd spent the whole three weeks wanting him badly, thinking of him as she masturbated each night. He pulled her towards him and sat her on his lap. Mike slid his right hand round her body to caress her breasts, while his left hand moved down her thigh. She was wearing a short thin cotton skirt, which he lifted and edged his fingers towards her panties. His prick was pressing eagerly between her buttocks; she pushed down hard against it. His right hand was inside her T-shirt now, playing with her right breast, her nipples were hot and hard. The urgency of her breathing pleased and excited him. Mike lifted her slightly so that he could undo his fly and free his cock, then he pulled her skirt up around her waist and firmly pulled her panties down just far enough over her thighs to leave her cunt exposed and accessible. With a clumsy movement Mike adjusted his position so that his penis was at the entrance of Monique's sex. Her cunt was dripping with juice, he grasped her thighs and pulled her down firmly, closing his eyes as his prick slid easily into her tight little pussy. He guided her cunt slowly upwards and watched his dick gradually emerge from inside her, right to the very verge of withdrawal, before slamming her back down on to his lap. Monique gasped as his cock rammed into her cunt.

"Shh," Mike whispered in her ear, speaking for the first time since he had begun touching her, "we don't want anyone to hear." He drove up into her cunt hard, again, and again, slapping her buttocks down on to his still-clothed hips. She stifled a cry. His eyes surveyed her body, enjoying the sight of her suntanned legs and the way her breasts jiggled beneath her T-shirt as the force of his thrusts shook her body. He felt Monique clench her buttocks, squeezing, making her pussy as tight as she could, though his prick was so big and hard it was already a tight fit. Mike was almost coming, but he didn't want the sex to end yet; abruptly he pushed her off him, stood up, went over to the door and locked it. When he turned, Monique had taken her panties off and was standing beside his chair humbly and expectantly, with her tight skirt still rolled up round her waist. Mike took her by the waist and turned her so that she faced the desk, then he bent her over, opened her legs a little wider, and let his probing penis find the entrance to her pussy, and squeeze itself back inside. He ran his hands up her back so that he could grip her shoulders, and as he did so, her T-shirt rose up and her heaving young breasts fell out, rubbing themselves against the blotter on his desk. He pushed into her, faster and harder, pressing her body into the desk. Harder and faster. Mike felt her body tense. He knew that she was about to come, although his prick had only been back inside her pussy for a few moments. The sensation was so strong and Mike felt the force of his spunk rising unstoppably. Releasing control he smothered a cry against the back of her neck and pinned her to him. His prick pulsated deep inside her as it propelled his cream inside her wanton cunt.

Almost immediately he withdrew and took a tissue from a box in his desk to wipe his dick, leaving her to pull her knickers back up and straighten her skirt.

"Don't worry about your marks, you'll be all right." Mike said. He wanted her to go now. Not that he hadn't enjoyed fucking her. But, he'd come back to the reality that she was only really interested in a good end of course report.

As he walked into class the next day his eyes went straight to Monique. He remembered with satisfaction how she had gasped and moaned when he brought her to orgasm. He felt better about himself than he had the previous morning, but the confidence of his younger days couldn't be fully restored by one fuck.

It was impossible to find out from Monique's expression what she was thinking. She seemed giggly and flirtatious, but whether she was laughing at him or with him he could not decide. It seemed to him too, that her friend was looking at him oddly as well. Clearly something had been said. Maybe they're laughing at me, he thought. Paranoia's set in he told himself; you're too old for this game. Anyway, he'd done what he'd promised. Monique's end of course mark now put her near the top of the class, he'd kept his part of the bargain. He was glad that today was the last day of the course.

When the lesson was over Monique came up to him. Mike busily shuffled his papers together.

"Mr 'ill," she began again.

"Try Mike it's easier," he suggested diffidently, without looking at her.

"Mike." She smiled, as if delighted by his name. "Mike, I wonder are you busy this afternoon?"

He looked at her quizzically. She had no need now, to be looking at him in a seductive way, she had got what she wanted. "Not particularly," he said.

"I shall be in my room," she smiled. "I shall look forward to you coming."

Mike was surprised but flattered by the invitation. He knocked on her door an hour later, looking around guiltily to see if he had been spotted. Male tutors were not supposed to go to the rooms of female students. The rules of the summer school were very clear on this point. The principal of the establishment, Miss Pitt, was a strict, starchy bitch and all the tutors were rather in awe of her. Mike did not relish being told off by Miss Pitt, but at that moment he was willing to risk it to find out if Monique wanted more of what she'd had earlier.

"Entrez," Monique called. He did so, and his heart sank when he saw that she was not alone.

"I 'ave invited my friend," Monique announced, "it is okay, I 'ope?"

Mike shrugged, "As you like," he said resignedly. Was she taking the piss, or what? He felt foolish standing there, but forced a smile nonetheless. Perhaps Tania wanted to improve her grades as well . . . In your dreams, he told himself. Monique was gorgeous, but Tania . . . she had to be the sexiest girl in the class.

"Well," Monique said, breaking the silence, "come . . please . . we fuck you?"

Mike looked from one to the other in dazed surprise, hardly daring to hope . . .

Monique led him to the bed. As he sat, Tania knelt between his legs, unfastened his trousers and gently peeled down his underpants to expose his erect penis. Mike caught sight of the glance that passed between the two girls, and smiled to himself; so young Bob couldn't compete in the size department! Tania lowered her head and ran her tongue teasingly round the tip of his penis, once, twice, and again, then she encircled it with her lips and began to suck. Drawing it into her mouth until her lips were buried in his pubic hair and the end of his prick was at the back of her throat. Monique was kissing Mike on the mouth caressing his lips with hers. Tania was slowly, sliding his penis out of her mouth, her lips gripping it firmly as it withdrew as if reluctant to lose an inch of it. Monique was perched astride his leg now, rubbing her sex against him, taking his hands she drew them up inside her blouse, against her breasts. Her nipples were as hard as pencil points, he took each one between his thumb and forefinger and squeezed, then began rubbing them, realising that he was keeping time to the rhythm Tania was setting as she sucked on his penis. Mike abandoned himself to the pleasure, laying back in the chair, and as if in a dream he saw Monique removing Tania's top and then her own. Tania's head sank lower and she began to lick his balls, very gently, while Monique reached down and took his prick in her hand, flexing her delicate, well-manicured hands round it as if getting used to the size of it before beginning to rub it rhythmically. Monique was still sitting on his knee, and Tania's hand crept up between

Monique's legs, fingering the lips of her cunt before fixing on her clitoris and starting to massage it. Mike's eyes bathed in the delectable sight. Feeling suddenly masterful, he pushed Monique's head down towards his cock and reached a hand out to each girl, pulling their bodies up on to the bed, one each side of him, and slipping his two hands into hot wet pussies. While one licked his balls and the other sucked on his dick, he finger-fucked them both firmly, and they responded, opening their legs wider so that his probing fingers could touch further inside to bring them more pleasure. There was no sound in the room except the steady rasp of their breathing. Monique was the first to come, and she took her mouth away from his cock as she cried out and buried her head in the bedclothes. Mike turned to Tania and pushed her towards the end of the bed so that her arse was right on the edge. Then he knelt on the floor between her legs and with his fingers pulled the lips of her cunt apart. Sitting back on his heels and surveying her sweet little pussy, he could not resist putting his mouth to it and flicking her clit a few times with his tongue. Then with the taste of her in his mouth, he sat up and ran the sides of his hands between her buttocks with his fingers caressing the slit of her cunt, rubbing the juices all over the insides of her thighs, so that her skin gleamed. Monique, herself satisfied, had rolled towards Tania and was licking her friend's nipples. An expression of rapture spread over Tania's beautiful face, and she stroked Monique's hair. Mike knelt on the bed and got behind Tania, pushing his cock into her welcoming pussy, then taking it out and teasing her with it, running it lightly over her clitoris. Whimpering, Tania moved her hand down and took his dick in her hand, rubbing it against her clit and then guiding it back towards her cunt. He pushed it deep inside her again, letting her have what she was aching for. She cried out with joy and orgasmed, drowning Mike's cock in the juices of her pleasure. Mike closed his eyes and thrust harder, faster, in pursuit of his own orgasm.

Suddenly the door swung open and there, framed in the doorway, stood Miss Pitt. Robed as usual in her black academic gown, she glared at the three of them. Tania quickly moved forward, pulling herself off Mike's cock to cover herself with the sheet. Unfortunately for Mike, he had reached the point of return, and jets of spunk spurted all over Tania's arse and back. There was nothing he could do.

"MR HILL! WHAT ARE YOU DOING?" boomed Miss Pitt. "And you two . . . you shameless tarts! Get your clothes on. Tania, clean yourself up! Have you no shame?"

"Miss Pitt . . I . . we . . we were just having some fun," stammered Tania.

Monique looked nervously at Miss Pitt, "You won't tell my father, will you, Miss Pitt, I beg you. I was only saying good-bye to Mister 'ill . ."

Miss Pitt was staring at Mike. His cock was still hard and he was trying to force it back into his trousers to do them up.

TEACHER'S PETS

"In my office, Mr Hill . . . NOW!" she ordered.

Mike fastened his fly and followed Miss Pitt down the corridor to her office. He knew what she was going to say; that behaviour like that will not be tolerated and furthermore, he had two hours to pack his bags. Did he care? Not much. Better to go out with a bang than a whimper he thought. And when Bob hears about it, he'll be green with envy.

They entered Miss Pitt's office. She closed the door behind them and turned the key. She went to sit behind her desk. Mike stood before her like a schoolboy.

"Well Mr Hill, what have you got to say for yourself?"

"If you're going to sack me get it over with. I've got no excuses. I was fucking two beautiful young girls, and I enjoyed every minute of it." Mike was surprised by his own forthrightness.

"And do you do this all the time then, Mr Hill?"

"Yeah. It's one of the perks isn't it? But you're a woman, you wouldn't understand."

"So, you don't think I have sexual needs Mr Hill? You don't think I would be interested in some meaningless sex then?"

Mike was confused. The conversation wasn't unfolding as he'd expected.

"No, I honestly don't think that you would," he said.

"Why - just because I'm a woman? Or because I'm the principal? Or maybe you think I'm frigid? Don't you think the sight of you fucking Tania turned me on? Well it did Mike."

Mike looked into her eyes. She was more beautiful than he had noticed before. Perhaps that was because she was talking about sex with him, instead of the syllabus and students' grades. He wondered what sex with her would be like. He had never thought of it before, she was usually so aloof. Was she just playing mind games with him? He tested her.

"What are you saying Catherine? That *you* want some sex, with me?"

She got up from her chair and walked to where Mike stood. Tracing her fingers across his chest, she looked into his eyes.

"You know that I've always liked you Mike," she said.

"I had no idea Catherine . ."

She began to unbutton his shirt, pulling it down off his shoulders and throwing it on the floor. Unclipping the top of his trousers and unzipping the fly, she slipped her hand inside. Mike's cock anticipated the touch of her hand and it pressed against her fingers as they stroked it.

"This is what I want Mike . . . I want your cock . . . I want it badly," she whispered as she began to massage his prick. "Those young girls always get the good fucks and I miss out. I want you to fuck me like you do them."

She pushed Mike against the edge of the desk. "Let me help you out of these," she said as Mike leaned back and Catherine pulled off his trousers and discarded them on top of his shirt. With one swift arm movement Catherine cleared the top of the desk of all its piles of paper and pens.

"Lie on the desk," she said firmly. Removing her gown. Mike did as he was told, enjoying her taking the control. His penis was clearly outlined pushing against his underpants. Catherine pulled the front of his pants down and took Mike's penis in her hand.

"Let me suck this for you," she said caressing its length. Then, leaning forward she placed her lips over its head and flicked her tongue back and forth. Mike could see down the front of her blouse, she wasn't wearing a bra and he could just make out a hint of nipple. Mike felt her warm mouth cover his prick. He couldn't believe the transformation in her. She couldn't get enough of him.

"Ooh, you're nice and hard, you like this don't you. I can taste the spunk oozing from your cock." She sucked a little more. "You'd better not come yet I want to feel it inside me," asserted Miss Pitt. "I'll get rid of these," she pulled Mike's pants down and tossed them on to the floor. "There, that's better." Mike was lying naked on her desk his prick fully erect, loving every delicious, unexpected moment.

"Stay exactly where you are, don't move. You think I'm a whore don't you . . . A bitch on heat?" Catherine said as she began to slowly take off her clothes. First she unbuttoned her blouse exposing her tits. She pushed one up towards her mouth and teased her nipple between her lips and tongue. "Oh, I'm so horny my nipples are as hard as bullets. I need your cock in my pussy, I'm aching for it. But first I'll have to gag you, that's what happens when you've been a naughty boy." Catherine tore a piece of sticky-tape from the dispenser and placed it across Mike's mouth. Then a second, and a third strip, so he couldn't talk. She then undid the zip at the back of her skirt and let it fall to the ground. Catherine was wearing stockings and suspenders, the stockings were sheer black nylon and the suspender belt was black lace. He was surprised that being gagged had made him even more excited. Catherine put one hand down the front of her panties and pushed a finger into her cunt. "Ooh, that feels good," she cooed. Then she turned her back to Mike, bent over, opened her legs slightly and pulled her panties down to her feet without bending her legs, giving Mike a clear view of her arse and pussy lips.

"Now I'm going to sit on your gorgeous prick. But first I want you to taste me." Catherine looked into Mike's eyes and fixed on them as she climbed up on to the desk and squatted over Mike's face, lowering her sex. "Oh you can't taste me, you've been a naughty boy haven't you. Well I'm not going to remove the tape." She sat on his face rubbing herself, covering him with her sex juices. Her eyes still watched his as she slid down his body so that her pussy lips were pushed against his erect penis. She leaned forward licking and kissing Mike tasting herself. "Mmm I taste so sweet, It's a shame you've been a naughty boy. Perhaps next time you'll leave silly young girls alone and come straight to a woman who knows how to treat a man." Catherine sat up. Taking his penis, she expertly guided it into her tight wet pussy. "Ooh yeah, that feels good doesn't it?

Suddenly Mike saw that they were being watched. Monique and Tania were staring at them through the window above the door and from the look on their faces they were horny as hell. Mike tried to tell Catherine, but he couldn't make himself heard above her gasps of delight. Anyway he could feel his prick was starting to twitch and his cum exploded up into Catherine's cunt. Feeling him come, Catherine rode him faster, rubbing her clitoris, feeling the force of her own orgasm rise. Her back arched, she pressed down on his cock as hard as she could, savouring every moment, until she collapsed with exhaustion on top of him.

Sitting up with his prick still inside her she ripped the tape from Mike's lips.

"Wow, that was some ride," he said. Catherine leaned forward and kissed him on the lips.

"Did you see Monique and Tania looking at us through the window above the door? I think they were getting off watching us. I don't think they could believe their eyes."

Catherine got off the desk and walked to the door. "No, I didn't see them. She said looking through the keyhole to the hallway. "Those little minxes are sex mad," she said as she turned the key and opened the door.

"Wait I'll come with you," Mike said hurriedly pulling on his trousers. "Aren't you going to put any clothes on Catherine?"

"No, there's no one left in the building now," she said. They walked down the quiet corridor checking the empty classrooms. Looking round the door of the last room they saw some large scrawled writing on the blackboard. It read 'MISS PITT SUCK COCK'. Monique and Tania were at the back of the room perched on the desks. Both had their hands in their panties fingering their pussies.

"You wait here Mike, I'm going to have some fun with these two," Catherine whispered. Mike did as she asked, and peered through the crack, wondering what she was up to.

Totally naked, she walked in the classroom. "Well, well, what have we got here? You two just can't keep your hands out of your knickers can you?" said Miss Pitt. As soon as they heard her voice they both stopped immediately; they were naughty schoolgirls who'd been caught doing something they shouldn't. "You two still have a lot to learn," Miss Pitt continued, picking up a piece of chalk. She put a line through their writing and underneath she wrote: 'MISS PITT SUCKS COCK'. Mike smiled to himself outside the door. "There that's the correct way to write it. I don't know what Mr Hill has been teaching you the last few weeks. And don't think we didn't see you spying on us, looking through the window. You really are a couple of nymphos. I've a good mind to tell your parents what you've been up to. In fact I think I will ring them right away."

"Please Miss Pitt, I beg you don't tell my father, he think I am a virgin," pleaded Monique.

"Well I can't think of a single reason why I shouldn't. Unless . . ."

"What . . . what can I do?" asked Monique.

"Well, I suppose I could set you a test. But you would both have to take it. If you pass it I won't tell your parents how badly you have behaved here. What about you Tania, will you help your friend stay out of trouble?"

Monique looked at Tania with hope in her eyes.

"Yes I will," said Tania softly.

"Come into my office and we'll see what you can do."

Mike dashed down the corridor and was sitting on Miss Pitt's desk when she came in followed by Tania and Monique.

"I thought you'd got lost Catherine," said Mike. "Oh I see you found the two peeping toms."

"Yes I found them masturbating in one of the classrooms. And one of them had written a rude remark about me on the blackboard," she said sternly. "I'm disappointed in them and I've told them I'm going to set them a final test. I want to see just how good their oral skills are. If they don't pass, I'll have to send a bad report back to their parents."

Monique and Tania looked sorry for themselves.

Miss Pitt paced a little as if deciding their fate.

"Don't worry girls," she said finally. "You're going to enjoy this test. You, Tania will perform oral sex on Mr Hill. And *you* . . ." Catherine stepped forward, looking deep into Monique's eyes, "you will perform oral sex on me. You will be marked on, technique, and visual presentation. Do you understand girls?"

BETTINA AND CANDY

Tania and Monique giggled and looked at each other. They nodded to Miss Pitt and said they understood.

"Mr Hill," Miss Pitt began again. "Lie on the desk please."

Mike didn't believe the situation in which he found himself. But, his penis was again straining against the inside of his trousers. He undid them and let them drop to the floor, stepping out of them he climbed back on to the desk and lay back, his hard cock resting on his flat stomach. He heard Catherine say "You may begin."

Tania and Monique were whispering together near the door. They began to remove each others clothes, they did this really slowly and sensually, caressing their bodies. Mike thought that they seemed really turned on by their task. When they were both naked except for their panties they walked over towards the desks where Mike and Catherine waited for them. Monique stroked Tania's hair and began to kiss her lips. Their mouths opened and their tongues explored deeply, while the bodies of the girls pressed against each other. Monique traced her fingers over Tania's breast, pausing at the nipple to feel its hardness and shape. Then her fingers slid down to Tania's pubic hair and began to tease her with featherlight circles around her pussy, promising to touch it but not doing so. Tania threw back her head. "Touch my pussy Monique," she said, pressing herself against Monique's hand.

Monique took away her hand. "Naughty girl," she reprimanded Tania. Then taking her hand she led Tania to Mike. "Here," she said laying Tania's fingers across Mike's erection. "Here is a cock . . . you must suck it good."

Tania began to stroke the length of Mike's shaft and it was huge and hard and hot under her touch. The girls' teasing was becoming unbearable, he wanted to be inside Tania's mouth.

Taking his penis in her hand she squeezed it gently. Then, without saying a word she leaned forward and slipped her lips over the tip of his prick and slowly took the entire length inside her mouth. She began to rock backwards and forwards her lips tightly slipping up and down Mike's shaft. It was bliss, and he struggled against his urge to come straight away. He looked over towards Catherine and Monique. Catherine was sitting in her chair with her legs spread wide apart. Monique was kneeling in front of her with her head buried in Catherine's sex. Monique had removed her panties and her arse was spread wide so that Mike could see her soaking pussy. Catherine was moaning and her breathing was fast, pushing her cunt into Monique's face. "Suck me," she cried. Monique withdrew teasingly and moved upwards to lick Catherine's nipples. She fondled them with her fingertips as she slid back down to press her tongue into the open pussy again. Catherine let out a cry of pleasure. Mike looked down to see Tania's lips eagerly sucking his cock and he could hold back no longer. His semen spurted out into Tania's mouth. She let the creamy consistency hit her tongue and hungrily she swallowed it, not losing a drop. Mike had never had such a powerful orgasm, whether it was Tania's young lips or seeing Monique eat Catherine's pussy he

BETTINA AND CANDY

couldn't decide, but he would have to give Tania ten out of ten.

Monique was still busy, feverishly working on Catherine's cunt. Monique's own juices were running down the inside of her thighs. Catherine screamed, lifting her bottom up and arching her back she roughly pulled Monique's head harder against her pussy.

"Yes, yes, lick me, suck me!" She cried.

Monique continued to press her tongue into Catherine's cunt, and Catherine opened her legs as wide as she could as she began to orgasm. She screamed out and grabbed Monique's hair, as the hot wet tongue darted around her pussy.

Catherine fell back exhausted into her chair.

Monique looked at Tania.

"Tania, my pussy ache, fuck me please." Monique begged. She was lying naked on the floor, pushing a finger between her sex lips. Tania quickly lay beside her friend and pushed three fingers into her cunt. Monique moaned, "More . . . yes . . yes." Then they were in the sixty-nine position, eating one another, drinking each other's sex juices. Tania was on top. Mike had never seen anything so sexy and his cock began to stir once again.

"I'm coming! Yes, now!" cried Monique. Her orgasm ripping through her body. Mike got behind Tania and clasping her buttocks, he eased his hard cock into her swollen cunt. Monique was still eating her as well and he could also feel her tongue on his penis as he thrust it in and out.

"Harder, harder!" shouted Tania. "Fuck me, fuck me

... Harder!" she screamed. "I'm coming!" Mike was still thrusting into her, and with one final thrust he came, ejaculating his spunk deep inside her. All three lay on the floor exhausted.

"I'll give everyone an A+," Miss Pitt exclaimed, laughing. "You've all passed with honours!"

Bettina writes,

My sister and I were always rivals, and we always competed for the attentions of boys when we were growing up. I remember once we almost came to blows over a boy called Charlie. It was a bit like a scene from the Jerry Springer show, 'My sister's stolen my man, and I want him back!' But blood's thicker than water so we both dumped him.

The following story is about such sibling rivalry and the lucky man in the middle is not complaining.

Sisters in Sin

SISTERS IN SIN

Jenny's mouth dropped open, eyes wide, as she saw them in the room opposite. It was *his* bedroom! Lisa was peeling off her T-shirt, writhing with pleasure as Tom's hands lovingly caressed her young firm breasts through her lacy black bra, squeezing her tits hard, as his mouth sought her nipples. His hands were inside the back of her panties, groping eagerly at her soft arse. Lisa pulled his head fiercely towards her own, pressing her lips to his. So engrossed in each other were the lovers that it seemed they gave no thought to the open blinds. The bra was gone now, and his mouth was sucking tenderly on her hard nipple. Lisa was in ecstasy.

What did her sister think she was doing in Tom's bedroom? She hardly knew him! Jenny thought about their conversation at breakfast where Lisa had berated her for thinking too much about boys, and told her it was a sin to go with a man before you marry. And look at *her*, the slut.

Jenny watched, hypnotized, as her sister's hand eagerly stroked Tom's crotch fighting with the zip. Suddenly, his rigid penis was exposed. Jenny's eye's widened at the size of it. To her it looked huge, and she wondered if she could handle such a monster inside her own tight little pussy? She looked longingly at Tom's muscular frame. He wanted her, she was sure of it; especially since she was a virgin and just sixteen. He was good-looking, and unlike boys her own age, knew what sex was all about. Perhaps she could steal him away from her sister and let him take her virginity. She knew he wanted to fuck her, although he tried to hide it.

Responding to her inner fire, Jenny ran her hands sensually over her young pert breasts, tweaking playfully at her nipples. They responded, growing harder, as she imagined his wet lips caressing them. Jenny felt her own hand forcing its way down her jeans, inside her already damp knickers. Her probing finger found the rosebud clitoris, begging to be stroked. She watched her sister's fingers wrapped around Tom's gloriously stiff cock, and gasped at the sight of Lisa taking it into her mouth eagerly, lips stretched around its girth. Jenny was trembling and licking her lips, sweat running down her face, her finger working so feverishly that it was hard to keep track of the lovers.

Soon Lisa was naked and Tom was kneeling in front of her, his tongue pressing into her sex. Jenny imagined Tom's tongue working away at her own wet pussy lips, instead of her sister's. Then Lisa fell backwards on to the bed, thighs parting invitingly, and her mouth was moving in invitation. Jenny bit her lip in envy, at the sight of Tom's handsome penis pushing its way insistently deep into Lisa's wet cunt. Jenny's finger suddenly seemed so inadequate as she pushed it in and out of herself. Her thighs began to tremble as she imagined herself straddling Tom's muscular legs. His strong hands squeezing her swollen breasts teasing her nipples. His rigid cock had her, unforgiveably speared, and she was faint with wanton lust, desiring nothing more than the feel of him exploding deep within her, taking what she so desperately wanted to give. Her fantasy had her grinding her hips mercilessly into his groin till she began to feel her orgasm. She threw back her head and closed her eyes as wave upon wave of pleasure ripped through her. Jenny's fingers were deep inside her pussy only her thumb exposed massaging her clitoris. When finally she opened her eyes the blinds opposite were closed. Had she been seen?

"Little bitch!" said Lisa as she closed the blind, her face flushed red from interrupted passion and anger at her sister. "Spying on us like some pervert would. Randy little cow. She's really winding me up. She's got it bad for you, and you encourage her . . ."

"Don't be daft love," replied Tom. "Let her be. If you rise to the bait she'll do it even more."

"I know you want to fuck the little bitch."

"I don't . . really I . ."

"You'd love to have her on this bed wouldn't you?"

Before Tom could answer, Lisa's hand grabbed his shaft. "She wouldn't know what to do with this . . not like I do." Suddenly she was wanking him off, biting at his ear and neck as his cock grew harder in response to her skilled fingers. He tried to grab her tits, but she brushed his hands away, sinking to her knees. Her left hand cupped his heavy balls while the right clasped the hot shaft firmly. Her mouth opened wide, and her eyes locked on his as the head of his penis shivered at the warm wetness of her eager mouth. She wanted to feel his spunk hitting the back of her throat, to taste it as she swallowed. He was helpless to resist her and he began to groan as his hot semen ejaculated into her mouth. Lisa sucked him dry. Nothing left for anyone else, she thought.

Tom opened his eyes and looked down. Lisa was licking her lips.

"Now I'll have to redo my lipstick," she said, "but it was worth it." He watched her dress and leave.

He looked out of the window across to Jenny's bedroom. He could see her lying on the bed looking at a book. She was so young and sexy and his mind filled with thoughts of her beautiful naked body, her large, young round breasts, her mouth begging to be kissed, her pussy aching to be fucked. His cock stirred once more. He tried to put away the thoughts of her, but he knew how easy it would be. She really had the hots for him and never tried to hide it. He was just imagining going down on her and taking her, when she looked up. She got up and came to the window. Opening it she called out, "Tom, Tom open the window."

Tom opened it and leaned out. "Hi Jenny," he said,

trying to be casual. He wondered how much of his earlier sex session she had seen.

"Tom, I need some help with this homework. Can I come over later? Perhaps after tea? I know it's something you could help me with."

"Okay Jenny, come over in about an hour. I'll look forward to it." I know what she wants, Tom thought, and it ain't algebra.

Jenny shut the window. Her pussy was wet again, this time with anticipation. She opened the top drawer of the dresser and carefully lifted out the giftwrapped box Tom had given her for her birthday. She lifted the lid, and still there, nestled inside the lingerie, was his note: *'When a girl reaches sixteen, she deserves things that make her feel like a woman.'* She pulled off her knickers and slipped on the matching bra and panties set of fiery red lace. She smiled as she remembered the moment she'd unwrapped it. Lisa had bitten her tongue, even though everyone could see she was furious with Tom for buying such an intimate gift for her.

Over the skimpy underwear she put on a short black dress. She'd borrowed it from a friend, because it emphasized her cleavage to perfection. She went downstairs to tea.

Lisa looked up at her from the kitchen table, and continued to glare at her while their mother passed between them, piling various sandwiches and cakes on the table.

BETTINA AND CANDY

Jenny sat down. She wasn't hungry and could only think of Tom, his face, his form, his huge hard cock . . .

Lisa interrupted her thoughts, "Are you okay Jenny? You seem distracted."

"I'm fine."

"I haven't seen that dress before."

"I borrowed it from Tania."

"It's a shame that it's not quite big enough for you," sniped Lisa.

"Tell me Lisa, what was it I saw Tom giving you earlier?"

Lisa glared some more, "Nothing," she said.

"But I saw you in his room . ."

"Girls, girls, can't you be nice to each other - just for once? Lisa, you know I've told you, you're not allowed to go in Tom's bedroom. He's a lot older than you . ."

"I wasn't in there Mum, there must be something wrong with Jenny's eyesight. Anyway what were you doing spying on Tom in his bedroom?"

Jenny felt herself blush. "I've got homework to do. I'm not hungry Mum," she said as she flitted the room

Tom was still at his window. He saw Jenny pick up some books and leave her bedroom in a flurry. He went downstairs and she was already on the doorstep, smiling coyly and adjusting her cleavage.

"Come on then love, come up."

Jenny followed him up the stairs and into the bedroom.

"Sit with me," said Tom.

Jenny sat next to him on the bed. Tom looked at her young body. Her full lips covered in lipstick he longed to lick off. His eyes fixed on her ample cleavage she 'carelessly' allowed him to see. Tom struggled with his aching need to possess her, his hard-on bulged in his jeans and threatened to rob him of all reason. But he knew deep inside that he wouldn't have invited her up to his room if he really didn't intend to fuck her. He just liked to think he was above sleeping with two sisters in one day. The reality was that he'd sleep with twins if he could.

"Tom," she whispered.

"Yes love."

"Will you help me with something?"

"Yes darlin' of course. What are you stuck on? Is that nasty teacher giving you a hard time again?"

"Oh, no, no .. it's nothing like that Tom. It's just that there are some things that I want to learn. And I know that you can teach me."

"I'm more your 'student of life' than an academic, you know Jenny," Tom said, smiling.

"That's exactly what I want from you Tom, your experience," she said, placing her hand tentatively on his fly.

Tom's cock pushed upwards, trying to force its way out of his jeans into her hand.

"Will you kiss me like you kiss Lisa?"

Tom felt his arm travel round her shoulders, his lips

touched hers and his passion for her erupted in deep probing kisses, as he fumbled to undo the zip at the back of her dress. It fell unwanted on to the floor.

"See Tom, I'm wearing what you bought me for my birthday. Do you like it on me?"

"Yeah, you look absolutely beautiful," Tom whispered. He ran his hands over the red lace of her bra, the nipples beneath stiffened till they were as solid as his straining penis, and he pulled the bra away.

Jenny could feel his enormous cock against her thigh as he ripped her bra down. She was awash with pleasure, revelling in the electricity of his every touch. His strong hands set her breasts on fire with their insistent caress, and her spine turned to jelly as his mouth fastened onto her pink nipple. Her hands frantically yanked down his shorts, grabbing eagerly at the throbbing heat of his erection. She was on her knees, desperate to feel its salty hardness between her lips. One hand cupped his hot balls, while her mouth moved up and down just as she had seen her sister do earlier that day. Her other hand was inside her wet panties working to relieve her sexual tension. Suddenly he pulled her head away, and pushing her on to her back, he ripped off the tiny pants. His head forced its way between her slim thighs. His tongue made her burn with the frantic need she felt, as it set fire to her soaking clitoris. Seconds later she felt the huge head of his cock touching her sex.

"Remember I'm a virgin! Don't hurt me too much," she said.

Then she felt the full length of him thrust into her. She hardly felt the slight pain, only pleasure that grew in intensity as the pumping of his actions had her head swimming. She cried out in ecstasy. Her legs locked themselves around his back and her hips rose and fell in time to his thrusting.

"Fuck me, fuck me, please! . . . . hard! . . . Harder!" she cried.

She could feel her passion rising and her orgasm overwhelmed her. Her pussy tightened around his cock and all at once he was filling her with a hot stream of spunk, pushing deep inside her with her every gasp.

Tom withdrew from her and lay back on the bed, his eyes closed. Jenny giggled, " That was wonderful Tom, now I know why Lisa's always round here. Tell me Tom, am I sexier than her?" Before he could answer Jenny began to kiss him, first on his lips, working her way down his body till her hot lips found his penis. She ran her tongue up and down its length till it was hard again. She knelt between his legs, one hand gripped the base of his shaft, while the other caressed his balls. Her tongue licked the head of his penis as it slid in and out of her mouth, her lips tightly clasped around it. Her hand rhythmically pumped the base of his penis and she could feel it start to convulse. Then suddenly hot cum ejaculated and filled her mouth with creamy spunk. Jenny pulled away abruptly, her mouth full and overflowing, as more jets of semen spurted on to her face and tits. She rubbed her fingers over her breasts to feel the warm juice as it ran down over and between them.

"Well Jenny, now I can answer your question. Don't breathe a word to your sister but if I was a horse racing man I'd say you won by a head."

Tom watched her dress and wiggle seductively out of his bedroom door, books under her arm. He sighed, smiled and shook his head, watching her gorgeous backside. He'd never felt so completely male, so good, and he'd be hanging on to it for as long as he possibly could. Sisters and sin. What a life!

Bettina writes,

This story is about two very naughty girls, and if I ever see them hitch-hiking I'll be sure to pick them up . . .

Back Seat Bitches

BACK SEAT BITCHES

Steve was sitting in a bar in Boulder when the two girls walked in. He could tell they were different, as they came close, he could hear them talking in French. The taller of the two was a Catherine Deneuve lookalike, blonde and willowy with green eyes, and the calm demeanor of an ice queen. The other girl had short dark hair, flirty brown eyes and a wide mouth that seemed to smile even in repose. The uncomfortable feeling that always came over him when he was in the company of beautiful women made Steve swing back to face the bar. But the girls came up alongside him and ordered two Cokes. They were still speaking French but kept giving him little sidelong glances. He knew because he was doing the same. Eventually, his gaze coincided head on with that of the dark-haired girl and she gave a small giggle. He smiled, acting more laid back than he felt, and made the kind of crass remark he always feared making.

"You girls new in town?"

He was sure that was enough to put them off, but the dark-haired girl looked at him and smiled.

"Just passing through, really," she said, in a sexy foreign accent. She pulled her hand out of the pocket of her tight jeans. "Hi, I'm Jeannie, and this is Belle."

He clasped her limp fingers automatically, but his mind was elsewhere. "Belle!" he repeated, staring into the ice queen's eyes so hard it must have seemed like he was counting the gold flecks in them. "Where are you from?"

"I'm from Quebec," Jeannie said, "and Belle is from Normandy, in France. We're here on vacation. We thought we might head into Denver tonight, then go on to Santa Fe to see some friends, but our car just broke down. They won't be able to fix it before tomorrow, so I guess we're stuck here for the night."

"Oh," he said, adding lamely, "well my name's Steve."

Jeannie looked as if she thought she might have given away too much. Belle just stared into the middle distance, with her long bare legs entwined around those of the stool. Her skirt was so short that Steve was treated to a glimpse of black panty. He wondered if she spoke any English.

"I could take you into Denver if you want," he heard himself say, steeling himself for the rebuff.

"That's real nice of you," Jeannie began, "but . . ."

Belle uncoiled her long legs from the stool and leaned towards Steve, the buttons on her tight fluffy pink cardigan gaping to show her black bra beneath. Something slowly unwound in Steve's stomach, generating a lot of heat.

"Thanks mister, we sure do appreciate that," said Belle.

He was taken by surprise. Her voice had a twang of the South about it along with the heavy French accent. It made her all the more intriguing. The full significance of her words didn't sink in until Jeannie echoed her, "Yes, that would be great. Thanks Steve."

"You mean you do want a lift?" The thought of taking these two lovely creatures into Denver in his clapped-out Ford suddenly struck Steve as ridiculous, but now he had to go through with it. The pair of them finished their drinks and followed him out of the bar. He saw every head in the place swivel in his direction and he felt the concentrated envy surround him like a cloud.

Steve was afraid they'd back out once they saw his car. The battered bodywork and rust around the door would be enough to put anyone off, but they didn't seem to mind. He opened the door for them and they both slid into the back seat, all thighs and calves, notching up his libido and turning him back into a randy teenager. Except that no girls of that calibre had ridden in his Oldsmobile way back when, in Oak Creek.

There was drizzling rain in the air as they set out, but as they passed the Victorians in the suburbs the rain turned into sleet, then snow. Huge flakes whirled around them in the air, and Belle squealed in delight.

"Oh, c'est comme Noel! It's like Christmas isn't it? White Christmas!"

"I love the snow!" Jeannie said. "I hope it gets real thick, so we can play in it."

"You won't be partying if it carries on like this," Steve said, all too conscious of being a party-pooper. "Roads can get treacherous round here. I'm not sure we should get on the highway."

He felt cool fingers twist the hair at the nape of his

neck, electrifying his spine, and a delicious French accent cooed in his ear. "Stevie! You wouldn't want to disappoint us now!"

"We'll take it easy then," he compromised. Steve reached for the radio dial. Belle poked his shoulder.

"Here Stevie, put this on for us." Belle handed him a CD, and he slotted it into the player. The girls squealed their appreciation and he felt better, even though he had to listen to Celine Dion for the rest of the trip. It was good to be around women again after weeks of being on his own and making do with self-help sex. He listened to Belle chattering away in French. He thought of the phrase 'to eat one's words' and fancifully imagined eating hers. It would be a gourmet experience; one where you would want to linger over each letter and savour the exotic flavour of every pronunciation.

By the time they reached the highway the snow was building up into drifts, but something about the girls' bright confidence uplifted his spirits, and he was oblivious to the possible danger.

"So thick, so fast they fall" Belle exclaimed, poetically. "May I open the window Steve? I want to let some of them fall on my tongue."

In the mirror he could see her, rapt and pale in the eerie glow from the street lights, her strawberry tongue dusted with snow-sugar. Jeannie put her arm around her friend and leaned out too, mouth open for the flakes to whirl in. They giggled and swallowed, shaking their heads to let the stray snow fall from their hair.

The snow was thickening now, doing a dervish dance around his windscreen and reducing visibility to a few yards. Steve was crawling along, aware that there was a long column of slow-moving traffic ahead, all caught unawares by the sudden downfall.

"Better close the window, keep the warmth in," Steve said, then wished he hadn't. Why did he have to sound like some grumpy old teacher with a couple of wayward kids?

Up ahead cars started to slew off the road. There were a couple of trucks too, stuck in drifts, and Steve grew anxious. He wondered how he had been stupid enough to attempt a trip on a night like this. He didn't want to alarm his passengers, but couldn't they see the danger they were in? Their French gossip and laughter was beginning to annoy him. Perhaps they were no better than a couple of dumb kids after all.

The snow was blowing hard all around, thickening into a solid blanket of pristine white. Steve calculated it would take them a couple of hours to get to Denver at this rate and he stepped on the gas a little. As the car glided askew everything went into slow motion and Steve struggled to recall what he had learned on the skid pan, but it all happened too fast for conscious thought. Within seconds the hood of the car was buried in six feet of snow and the rear wheels were turning in thin air.

"Fuck it!" he swore, as the engine died. There was no sound from the back. A glance in the mirror showed two dumb struck faces out of a B-movie thriller.

BETTINA AND CANDY

"Are we in real trouble?" Jeannie asked, her voice trembling a little.

"Guess so," Steve said, as he tried to rev the engine, but it was dead.

"What do we do?" Belle asked.

"We sit tight and wait for the snow to thaw, or the tow truck to arrive, whichever happens first."

"Oh my God!" Jeannie said. "Will we have to stay here all night?"

Steve didn't answer. Celine's voice died away into silence; the profound silence of a world soundproofed by snow.

The girls started to chatter in French, their voices subdued as if they were in church. Steve leaned back in his seat and closed his eyes. There was some gum in the glove compartment, but nothing else to eat or drink.

There was a rustling from behind, and before Steve could turn around, something was binding his upper arms, a long silk scarf that smelt of the perfume one of the girls was wearing. They'd taken him completely by surprise, imprisoning him in his seat, and he was too stunned to even wriggle. There were giggles as fingers struggled to tighten the knot at his back.

"Hey, what do you girls think you're doing?"

Steve struggled then but found he couldn't escape his tight bondage. He cursed, wondering what the hell they were up to. Wasn't their situation bad enough already?

"We just don't want you to interfere with what we're doing," Jeannie said firmly.

"What the hell are you doing?"

"We have to keep ourselves warm somehow. We could get what d'you call it? Hypo . . ."

"Hypothermia." stated Steve. "Look, you won't freeze to death. Not if you stay in the car. Untie this thing will you?"

Steve put his hands up but the girls were too quick for him. Jeannie grabbed his wrists, and Belle tied another scarf around them, with surprising efficiency.

"You pair of fucking bitches. I give you a lift and this is how you treat me!"

"It's for your own good Steve," Jeannie cooed. "Now be a good boy and stay quiet. And DON'T look round."

Steve sat still. He wondered what they were up to. He had nothing that they'd be interested to steal, except his car, and that was out of action. Not that they could go very far. He had no money to speak of, just a fist full of dollars. He thought it best to stay quiet and sit it out.

"Find some music on the radio Jeannie, something sexy," said Belle.

Jeannie leaned over the passenger seat and turned the dial, finding some cool jazz. Steve faced front and tried to calm himself. Whatever they were up to didn't seem to involve him. After a few minutes he heard noises from the back seat. It sounded like the girls were making love. Perhaps he was misinterpreting the sounds, but he was sure it was kissing and heated breathing. He was tempted to turn around to see, but was afraid of what they might do to him if he did. There was a rustling of clothes, and a clunking of shoes on the floor. Steve leaned back and closed his eyes. Those horny bitches he thought, as he imagined what they might be doing, to themselves, and to each other. He heard wet gasping sounds and visualized them kissing, their hands exploring each others breasts. It wouldn't take much to get into Belle's bosom with her cardigan half unbuttoned and her black bra showing. He could see her cleavage, plump and pale, and he imagined that her nipples would be small, hard and pink once they were exposed to the air.

Steve's cock stirred in his pants as the girls started to moan. He opened his eyes and shifted in his seat to try to get a view of them in the mirror. At last he could see. Both girls were stripped to the waist and caressing each others' breasts. Belle's were firmer than he'd imagined and with larger, darker nipples. Jeannie's were pinker, tight and puckered, sitting pretty on trim little tits. Steve watched. Jeannie took one of Belle's nipples between her lips and sucked it and licked it. Belle's short skirt was hitched up around her waist to expose her belly button, pierced by a silver ring. Jeannie's hand pushed its way into the front of Belle's panties, and as the fingers slipped underneath her crotch, Belle leaned back to allow more access. She exclaimed some French words and Jeannie fingered her some more. Jeannie pulled out her sticky forefinger and licked it, slowly, "Mmm you taste good," she sighed.

Belle began unzipping her friend's jeans, helping her out of them. Then she slipped her hands around Jeannie's curvaceous backside. They kissed passionately and their bodies pressed together as they wriggled.

"Que j'ai chaud!" Belle exclaimed, as they both came up for air. Jeannie opened one of the back windows and the snowy air began blowing around in the car, frosting Steve's face with ice kisses.

"Hey, are you crazy?" he called. They ignored him.

"Oh that lovely cold stuff!" Belle said. "Take a handful, Jeannie. I want it on my tits! Rub me with it . . oh yes!"

Steve watched as Jeannie massaged the snow on to Belle's nipples. His erection pressed against his fly.

"How ya doing Steve?" Jeannie taunted.

"Fuck you!"

"Now that's no way to speak to a lady." Jeannie reached out the window and grabbed another handful of snow. Then she leaned over his shoulder, unzipped his fly and filled his crotch with freezing stuff. He yelped.

"That should cool your ardour boy," she said, and gave a sadistic laugh. "We don't want you getting too excited."

They went back to their erotic pursuits, breathing heavily. Jeannie was licking the melted snow from Belle's nipples, warming them again with her mouth. Both girls were fingering each other, their lithe bodies entwined, their legs apart.

Recovered from its icy shock, Steve's erection was soon full blown again, buoyed up with the hope that they would eventually let him join in. His balls were lying heavy in their sac and a slow heat was spreading through him, despite the rapidly chilling air and the pool of dampness at his groin.

The girls shut the window and it went very quiet for a while as they kissed sweetly. They had slid down in the back seat and he could see Jeannie's arm moving up and down. He strained his neck to see what they were doing. His cock twitched like a dowsing rod attuned to sexual energy instead of water. Belle held Jeannie's tits in her hands and was squeezing them gently. He followed Jeannie's arm down to see what her fingers were doing. Then he could see she held a dildo. It was disappearing inside Belle's pussy and then gently out again. The motion had Belle wriggling and soft-sounding, pretty French words escaped from her lips. Jeannie leaned forward and kissed her friend deeply, her tongue delving into Belle's mouth as the dildo disappeared inside her cunt.

Steve desperately wanted to relieve his bursting cock. He moved his arms around and tried to release his bonds. Finally he managed to pull out one wrist from the ties, and he immediately slid his hand down to his erection. He took his cock in his hand but the girls noticed his movements. They grabbed his arms and Jeannie bound his wrists once more. He heard the window open again and arms pushed down his body.

"Hey . . . what?" he began.

Steve's underpants were pulled right open and, before he could protest, handfuls of snow were once again thrust into them. He yelped as his cock and balls received a dunking of ice, sending spasms of pain and shock spiralling through his body, making his dick shrink instantly.

The girls giggled. "That will teach you," Jeannie said. "You need to cool down. And you need to mind your own business."

"You bitches!"

Their laughter turned into small cries of satisfaction as they resumed their love-making. Steve felt the sodden underpants clinging to him and desperately wanted to remove them. Anger was threatening his determination not to provoke those back seat bitches any more than necessary. Trust him to pick up a couple of dykes. For the first time it struck him that he might suffer real harm if Jeannie persisted in her spiteful douches. What if he caught pneumonia? What if . . .?

"Mon Dieu! Vite, plus vite! Ah, c'est meilleur!"

Belle's voice expressed the unmistakable urgency of a woman in orgasm. Her gasps were filling the car. Steve imagined the back seat obscured by a sexual miasma and his erection returned slowly, filling him with relief. He'd feared his penis might have been so traumatised it would never rise again. By using all the strength in his fingertips, he managed to push his pants right down under his balls, letting the air get to his cock.

Steve conjured up an image of the two girls in disarray, bodies twisted so their mouths could reach each others' pussies, breasts flopping out of their bras with ice hard nipples. His erection thickened and lengthened, rising into the space created by pulling down his pants, feeling more comfortable now the window was closed and the air warm. He gave a deep sigh and stretched back into his seat, wondering just when, or if, his turn would come. Jeannie's voice echoed in his ear. "Harder, Belle!" Steve's cock responded to the command. Both women were gasping. His balls stirred heavily in the sodden gusset, building their load. It was heavy weather in all senses. The subzero climate outside the car contrasting with the tropical atmosphere within, as the girls laboured for their fulfillment. Steve drew himself up and strained forward, until his view in the driving mirror was again widened. He could see Belle stretched out on the seat with her knees up, Jeannie's tongue pressed into her friend's pussy. Belle's hand disappeared between Jeannie's thighs. He couldn't see her fingers but her arm moved gently up and down. The girls were hot, flushed and sweaty, their breasts half out of their tops, receiving the odd casual caress to keep their nipples in full bloom. Steve's hands dropped to his lap, and he began to flick across his exposed glans with his fingertips. It wasn't enough, but it was something.

Steve squinted at the girls, watching them wriggle and flush as they raced towards climax. Who would arrive first? Even when aroused, Belle looked pale as vanilla ice-cream while Jeannie was glowing. Hot French toast and champagne sorbet. Mmm! He breathed in the sweet aroma of their sex, and began rubbing just below his glans where he was most sensitive. Jeannie reached orgasm and screamed out as it overcame her. Soon Belle was coming again too. Although more restrained than her friend, she threw back her head to expose her long white throat, shuddering convulsively. Steve ached for relief. How much more could he take?

Sitting bolt upright, with an intent expression, Jeannie appeared to be listening to something. Looking round, Steve could see the floodlit road, and a huge snow plough cutting a swathe through the snow. Following on behind was a tow truck and a string of other vehicles. The two girls stared out of the rear window for a few seconds, then began to dress rapidly, combing their hair and touching up their make-up.

"Hey you two, untie me. . ."

But then, both girls were scrambling out of the car, pushing through the powdery snow towards the convoy of cars and trucks.

Steve watched as the girls approached a sleek black Ford parked on the highway. He saw their shadowy figures, Belle fixing her hair, and Jeannie bending over to talk to the driver who had wound down his window. The back door opened and the girls jumped in.

Bettina writes,

When I was last in the States, I checked out some strip bars. I like to watch the exotic dancers. One of them really turned me on. Her name was Candy. She had more money in her g-string than any of the other girls, and the most exquisite figure, breasts you would die for, and luscious thick, wavy blonde hair.

She was so sexy I asked for her to do a private dance for me. It was $20 and worth every cent. There was a 'no touching' rule, but Candy took my hands and rubbed them up and down her body as she danced. She was totally naked except for her g-string and high heels. She told me to wait for her till she'd finished her set. We both knew there was a spark between us, a sexual chemistry that was electric.

Candy loves working in the sex industry, and I've included this interview I did with her just after we met, because she's never afraid to be honest about herself and her life.

The Interview

THE INTERVIEW

I arranged for Candy to come to my room at The Edison Hotel in Manhattan. We'd only known each other for a couple of weeks, and I was eager to get into her mind (as well as her panties!) I planned for it to take the afternoon, but it turned into a long weekend. We made good use of room service, and the bottles in the mini-bar.

This is a transcript of the tape I made.

B.V. Candy, what was your first sexual experience, and how old were you?

C.L. Oh let me see, oh yes, I must have been about fourteen. I'd already kissed a couple of boys, but this was my first memorable sexual experience. I stayed over at a girlfriend's house. Her name was Chloe. You know what girls are like. We couldn't sleep, all we talked about were boys and well, we both got turned on. I don't remember how it began, but we started playing with each other. Oh, I know, she had some condoms that she'd stolen from her parents' room. She went to the kitchen and brought back this huge carrot. We put the condom on the carrot and pretended it was a dick. First we just mucked about with it. But we ended up fucking each other with it. It was my first orgasm with another person, and I've loved carrots ever since!

B.V.   Did you eat her pussy?

C.L.   No! I don't know what it's like in England, but at fourteen I wasn't ready for that! We just fingered each other, and masturbated with this huge carrot. I can remember that when I came I made so much noise her mother came into the room to see what was going on. Luckily she knocked first so we were able to cover ourselves with the bedclothes. We pretended we'd been having a pillow fight! But I think she knew what we'd been doing.

B.V.   What about boys?

C.L.   Well, I was into boys from an early age. I've always been an exhibitionist, and I can remember in my early teens, in the playground, I used to lift my skirt for boys and show them my knickers if they gave me fifty cents. It was an early forerunner to my lap dancing!

B.V.   When did you lose your virginity?

C.L.   When I was fifteen. I was at a party, it was my friend Sandy's sixteenth birthday party. I was dancing with her brother, Ricky. He was about eighteen, and really good looking. He was touching me all over my ass and be-

THE INTERVIEW

tween my legs and I was getting really hot and horny. The party was in like a huge apartment on one floor with lots of rooms leading off a corridor. We sneaked to his bedroom, and there were piles of coats on his bed. As I was moving them aside, he was pushing up my dress and pulling down my panties, he couldn't wait to get it inside me. It hurt a bit at first, but then it felt nice. It was over pretty quickly though! I didn't see him again. I had a few boyfriends after that who didn't know what they were doing when it came to sex. Then I met Dale, and we went steady for a year, till he moved away. He was experienced and I learned a lot from him about sex. You know, that it didn't have to be over in seconds!

B.V. Was he older than you?

C.L. Slightly. I was seventeen and he was about nineteen when we met. But he'd had lots of girls I think, though he told me he hadn't.

B.V. So sex with him was good?

C.L. A revelation! We'd have fucking sessions in my bedroom when my parents were out. It would last for ages and he really knew how to arouse me which other boys I'd been out with had no idea about. He encouraged me to use my tongue on his dick. I wasn't sure how to at first of course, but he gently guided me and I learned how to really turn him on and please him with my mouth. And since I've been in porn films and stuff I've developed my technique even more.

B.V.   How did you get into the sex industry?

C.L.   Well as I mentioned before, I'm an exhibitionist. I love being in front of the camera, posing for a photographer, or being filmed. And I love to have men look at me and get turned on by me. So when a photographer gave me his card and asked me to model for him I was really pleased. I'd just broken up with Dale as he went to Idaho to live. I was really pissed at him for going. He knew I couldn't leave my studies. I thought it would cheer me up to do some posing, so I went to the photographer's studio. He gave me some red and black underwear and a blouse and skirt to put on. He said just a bit of the underwear showing would look really good. So I put on the blouse and skirt over this skimpy stuff and stood in front of the lights. He had like a little set of a chair and a dressing table with a lamp on it. I sat on the chair and he took some shots. Then he told me to unbutton the blouse a bit, to show some of the bra. And then he arranged my skirt up my thighs a bit and told me to slightly open my legs so a bit of my panties was showing. He said I looked really good and encouraged me, so I started to pose without his guidance. He said it was great and could I just slip the skirt off so I'd just be wearing the blouse and the panties and bra. I thought why not, I was enjoying myself. He was clicking away and I peeled off the blouse, and slipped the straps of the bra down over my shoulders. Well you know I've got big tits, and I thought to myself is this for some good shots or is he just getting off on it, but I didn't care either way! I turned my back to pull off my bra looking back over my shoulder at the camera. Then I turned to face him with my hands on my tits and my hair falling forward and he loved it. I think he was surprised I was so confident on my first shoot. He thought I'd modelled before. After that I posed for him regularly. My next step towards the sex industry came when I was still a student actually. I needed the money, so I got a job as a waitress in a bar where there were topless dancers on little stages. I'd been there a few weeks and I was watching the dancers one night and I thought to myself, I can do that, and a whole lot better than they can! So I told the boss that I wanted to try it. I got up and he told the guys in the bar it was my first time taking off my clothes and dancing. They loved it! They whistled and cheered. I danced really well, slowly stripping off my clothes down to my panties. I really teased them and I got lots of tips, more money than I usually made in a week. After that, dancing and stripping was what I was really into.

B.V. So you get turned on by it?

C.L. Oh yeah! Some guys are really hot, and I dance really close to them, but I don't let them touch me. Then I start to imagine them sinking their dicks into me. It makes me dance better when I think about sex.

BETTINA AND CANDY

B.V. Do you ever have sex with the bar guys?

C.L. I have done in the past, but I usually make a rule not to. The one I most remember was when I danced for this guy who was real quiet and elusive. He didn't show any kind of reaction to me at all. I was attracted to that. He was at the bar for quite a few nights. When I left work I noticed him sitting in a big car right outside. He looked at me, and instinctively I just got in. It was stupid really, you never know who you are getting in a car with do you? But I just had this desire for him, probably because I didn't feel like I'd turned him on yet and I wanted to. I sat beside him and he didn't say anything. He unzipped his fly and he had no underwear on, just a huge hardon that poked upwards through the open zip. I knelt on the seat and bent forward over his cock, he pushed it upwards towards my mouth, and I just took it in.

B.V. You gave this guy you'd never met before a blow job in his car?

C.L. Yeah. I know it's crazy. I wanted to arouse him, and I wanted to feel it grow larger and harder in my mouth as he got more excited by what I was doing to him. I sucked on his dick till he came in my mouth. I never saw him again.

B.V. So, you like giving oral sex, what about receiving it? Does anyone get to eat Candy?

C.L. I think I may have heard that one before! Yes they do. I particularly like girls to do that for me. I love to look down and see a girl between my legs sucking my pussy. I quite often do girl-girl shoots, where we pretend to do it. We have to do it in a visual way where the camera can see everything, like the tip of her tongue on my clit. But sometimes I do videos, and then we often really do the whole thing till I come. If I can I take the girl home with me, but if I can't, then when I get home I masturbate and think about her. I did a particularly horny shaving video with a girl called Rena. We were filmed in this huge bathroom and we were sitting on the floor. I had on some white stockings and a short dress, but no panties underneath. She had to say to me 'I'd love to shave you, would that be ok?' and I replied 'yes'. She lifted her skirt and showed me that she was completely shaved. 'Shall I shave you completely bare like this? and I said 'yes'. Then she pushed my dress up to my waist and parted my legs gently. She ran her fingers up my thighs to the top of my stockings. It felt great and I started to get wet with anticipation. I always make a ritual of shaving anyway so to have this cute chick do it for me was really erotic. Taking the shaving cream she squirted it into the palm of her hand. With her fingertips she spread the cream over my pubic hair and around my open pussy. It was cold and smooth and felt luxurious. She took the razor and dipped it into some warm water in a big metal bowl. Then slowly she shaved me and I kept really still and the razor glided over my public bone. She said, 'Spread your legs more so I can do around your pussy hole.' These words were meant to get the video viewers more aroused of course but they really made me horny! After she had finished, she poured water over my pussy from a little cup, and it dripped down over my clit and on to the floor. By this time I needed her tongue down there real bad! Then she pressed her hands against my open thighs and went down on my newly shaved pussy. To feel her face against my smooth pussy and her lips and hot tongue delving into my hole was just something else. Can you imagine?

B.V. I think we'll take a break now!

I stopped Candy there as I was feeling too hot to handle. I was imagining everything as she was describing it, and the thought of her with the shaving girl had my panties soaked and sticking to my pussy. I went to the bathroom to change them, as you know reader from 'Erotica 1' that I always carry plenty of spare pairs! Then I got us both a cool drink and resumed our discussion on videos ....

B.V. So, you were telling me about shoots and videos where you often perform with other girls . . .

C.L. Oh yes. I did a shoot last week with Leyna. She's

a girl I work with a lot as we look good with our different hair colors. We're doing a lot of bondage at the moment as there is a big demand for it. Leyna played the role of a dominatrix wearing tight shiny black clothes, and she had a whip and a cane for some of the shots. I was naked and she had to restrain me with ties that bound my wrists, and a bar tied to my ankles that kept my legs apart. The photographer said he wanted it to look like an Eric Stanton cartoon, really graphic and full of action. Leyna tied me up really tightly, and then I leaned over a chair and she spanked me. I really got into that. And the make-up artist put some red marks on my ass with blusher to make it look like I'd really been spanked hard. Then while I was still tied up, Leyna teased me and licked my pussy. It was so erotic. I love playing those roles for shoots. It's a fantasy that you can act out.

B.V. So you enjoy domination fantasies then?

C.L. Yes. I love being dominated by another woman. I saw a TV program recently about a dominatrix and her slave. This girl loved to be submissive and she was bending over a table while the dominatrix whacked her bare ass with a whip. These marks were real and they were getting redder and redder, and the girl still asked to be whipped. I was getting so turned on by it I started to masturbate while I watched. Then the girl said a word that they'd agreed would be the signal that she'd had enough. The dominatrix took her to a mirror to look at her own red backside. Then the girl was tied to a table by a female helper of the dominatrix. The helper held the girl's arms down against the table above her head while the dominatrix pierced the girl's nipples with sharp silver pins. It must have really hurt and the dominatrix said she'd been a good girl because she didn't cry out.

B.V. Did that turn you on too?

C.L. Yeah, but I wouldn't let her do it to me!

B.V. So do you prefer the photo shoots to filming?

C.L. Filming takes a lot longer than shoots, and there can be some waiting around, but I do enjoy the flow of action and the free flow of it all. Last month I did some videos for a company that sells a lot of stuff on the internet. I had three sex scenes to do for the short films. The one I enjoyed most was with this guy called Barry. He was particularly nice to me and wants to take me out to dinner. That's the porn industry, sex first, dinner later! He and I filmed a scene where he fucked me from behind, you know, doggy style. I love that position, and he pulled my hair too, which totally turns me on. I love having my hair pulled, don't you? Especially when I'm giving a blow job to a guy and he is pulling hard on my hair. Anyway, the second scene I did was with Rachel. I'd met her before as she does a lot of porn. They had the camera close up on my pussy and they wanted to get real close shots of her pushing a dildo inside me. She has lovely long nails painted with bright red varnish so they look really good up close. She pushed the dildo inside me and then began to rub my clit with her fingertip. It felt so good and I had to stay real still as the camera was fixed in one position. The dildo was sliding in and out and I just came, and tried to keep still at the same time. It was intense! Then finally, I had sex with this guy, I don't know his name, and then I had to kneel in front of him while he wanked himself off into my mouth and over my face. They wanted to get a close up of my face covered in his cream. Then they edited it down to a 10 second 'cum shot' for the internet. It's out there on the web somewhere! It's like a taster of what's on their videos, if that's the right word.

B.V. Sounds like the exact right word to me!

C.L. I had to let it come back out of my mouth instead of swallowing it so it could drip down my chin.

B.V. Do you usually swallow it, then?

C.L. Yes if I feel like it? Do you Bettina? Do you spit or swallow?

B.V. Hey, I'm asking the questions!

At this point in the interview we took another break. We

BETTINA AND CANDY

had some lunch, and I found it difficult to eat because I was so turned on. I kept imagining Candy going down on me, I couldn't help myself. The images kept coming into my mind, and I suppose I didn't try that hard to push them away! My panties were soaked again. When we began again, I thought I'd press Candy more about what turns her on ...

B.V. Candy, what other kinds of things make you hot and horny?

C.L. I did a film with Leyna and her boyfriend Dan last year. It was only an amateur thing, with this guy called Jed filming us with his hand held video camera. Jed had some really good ideas. When I did a blowjob on Dan, Jed told me to hold the cum in my mouth, and then drip it into Leyna's mouth and kiss her. It was so fucking erotic and looked great on film, even though Jed wasn't the best cameraman in the world. The footage was shaky at times, even slightly out of focus, but that all added something. It had that kind of homespun feel to it, spontaneous kind of thing. I remember Jed had this enormous erection sticking out of his trousers. He was really getting off on directing us. His wife was watching through the upstairs window. She must have been getting hot as well, because after he'd stopped filming she came down and took his dick in her mouth right in front of us. She didn't care! I love that.

THE INTERVIEW

B.V. So, you don't mind working with amateurs then?

C.L. No, as long as I've met them, and I think that they're genuine, and they've got good ideas. I won't work with them if I think they just want to look at me with my legs wide open! They've got to be into creating something good. I learned that when I first started out. When I was modelling I met some real jerks. But I also met some inventive people who I work with a lot, because they are exceptional. They may not have a lot of money to throw around, but they have imagination, and you can't buy that.

B.V. So creating something good is the most important thing?

C.L. Yeah, and having a good time doing it?

B.V. And who has inspired you?

C.L. Well, anyone who gets out there and does what they want, and doesn't care what other people think. I mean in an artistic way, not violence and stuff. It can take a lot of guts to say this is me, this is what I do, and fuck you if you don't like it. I saw this guy on TV once as I was flicking through the channels late one night. You know, how you do when you're bored, with nothing to do. Well, this guy was being interviewed in the back of a limousine. He was with this really hot chick with flaming red hair. I think they were in a band or something. The interviewer asked him about success, and he said, 'We became successful doing what we love, and that's the only way you can be a success'. And I thought about it and realised he was right. Those words stuck in my head and I have always done what I wanted to do since then.

B.V. So what kind of things would you like to do that you haven't done yet?

C.L. You mean work ambitions or fantasies?

B.V. Tell me about both.

C.L. Well I'd love to make my own films and I plan to do that one day soon. Perhaps you could star in one of them Bettina? I'd love to direct sex scenes and film them myself. Telling the girls exactly what I want them to do would be a real turn-on, and ordering guys to put their dicks in the girls mouths or into their pussies, well it gets me all horny just thinking about it! And I have many, many fantasies that I haven't done yet! One in particular I think about is lying on the floor, with all these guys around me wanking off over me. I've done it with two guys when I was filming. I was kneeling and they were standing and I gave them oral sex, you know alternately, going from one dick to the other and back again till they came. And when they did they both ejaculated over me, over my breasts. But in my fantasy, there are at least ten men around me,

THE INTERVIEW

and I'm lying naked on the floor. They wank themselves off and their cum spurts all over my body and into my open mouth, and I'm covered in it. Then I rub it all into my breasts and my pussy. Sometimes I think about this one when I'm masturbating and I use some food like cream or vanilla yoghurt to pour on my body, over my tits, and between my legs. It feels very sensual even though it's not the real thing.

B.V. Will you put that scene into one of your films?

C.L. Yeah, and I'll make sure I'm starring in that one!

B.V. And other fantasies?

C.L. Well, when I work with girls we often use double-headed dildos, or strap-ons. I like to have a girl fucking me with a strap-on, as I can squeeze her breasts and fondle them and she can do the same to me and we can kiss, and I still get the feeling of having something deep inside my pussy at the same time. What I'd love to try is having a guy underneath me with his cock inside me, and a girl behind me with her strap-on dildo up inside my ass. I would be sandwiched between them getting both holes filled at the same time. I've seen other girls doing it in films but I've never done it myself yet.

B.V. Well, we look forward to seeing that one Candy, when it comes out on video! Thanks for giving us such an intimate interview.

C.L. Thanks Bettina. Hey are you feeling horny?

> ... *sshh .. click ... The tape ran out.*

Candy writes,

This is my most favorite story. I love it so much that I have read it over and over, and every time it arouses me so much - I still haven't managed to read the end!

Bettina:
You really are a naughty girl Candy, I think you deserve a spanking.

Candy:
Don't start me off again!

Spanking

SPANKING

Slowly Mary turned to accept his kiss, her eyes closed, savouring the moment. His hand moved down to trace the roundness of her backside, but she was shocked when, almost before she was aware, his grasp had found her naked flesh, and gasping, she knew then that whatever he did she would be unable to resist.

She had wanted a gentle embrace, but now she leaned into his rough insistence as he pulled her to him and his fingers sought the spot she now longed for him to touch.

She heard herself say, "Take me. Use me." Though she did not dare articulate what she really wanted from him, she hoped now he might guess.

Suddenly he pulled away, leaving her dress rucked up. She turned slightly, aware that her buttocks were exposed, her pants now pulled tight. Gently, he turned her around by the shoulders, and she could almost feel his appraising eyes drop down.

She heard herself saying: "You can do anything you like, you know," and it sounded lame and arch. She thought she'd destroyed the mood, but he said, "Anything?" And as his hands caressed the full globes of her bottom, she leaned against them. I can't spell it out, she thought.

As her mind wandered for a moment, suddenly there

was a sharp crack and a sharp sting of pain. Though she wanted to cry out, she merely breathed in sharply, and waited.

His aim on the other cheek was lighter, quicker, and she felt it quiver before a much subtler and exquisite stab of pain fanned out.

"More?" he asked quietly.

"Yes . . . no . . . just take me . . . now!"

As he entered her, she was wetter than she had ever remembered, and he was fucking her, hard and fast. He came suddenly, before she could, and though she felt unfulfilled by the sex, the warmth suffusing her backside took over, making her yearn for more sex, or more spanking, it didn't matter which.

They fell back on the bed and she took his penis in her hand. There was no reaction. She eased herself off the bed.

"Just wait there," she called over her shoulder as she left the room.

She returned, ready to put her tennis gear to a use she had only ever fantasized about. It was the shortest skirt she had, and it was bright white. With white socks, white pumps and a white T-shirt, the outfit, despite its colour, had associations that were far from virginal.

She scratched her bottom idly, teasing him, aware that he couldn't tell from where he stood whether she was wearing knickers, or not. She was. She figured the more there was to take off, the better. He opened his mouth to say something, but she motioned him to be silent.

"I'm not quite ready for my tennis lessons, sir," she said meekly. "I've got to do up my laces first." An excuse for an elaborate pantomime of turning her back and bending over leisurely to tie her shoes. With her legs straight as she bent over, her little skirt rose up to reveal white cotton panties.

She stood upright again and looked at him coyly. "I'm sorry I'm so late for my lesson. I never do seem to be able to arrive on time." She looked him straight in the eye. "I haven't been practising my forehand like you told me to either." Her eyes wandered down to below his waist, and wondered whether her little act was having the desired effect.

"Well you obviously need an incentive young lady. I suggest that you untie those laces again, take the pumps off, and bring one over to me."

"What do you intend to do?"

"Something to concentrate the mind."

She brought one of the shoes over and handed it to him. He sternly told her to hold her ankles. She did so. He pulled up her skirt, tucking it into the waistband, revealing a large pair of white cotton school knickers. He started to ease them down, but she squeaked, "No, don't, not on my bare bottom."

"Take this in silence then, or they're coming off soon enough."

The slipper didn't really hurt, for he was obviously

not sure how painful it would be and how hard he should hit her. But just in case he was stopping at six, she cried out at five. Suddenly his feigned anger sounded terribly convincing. She felt very aroused.

"Take the knickers down," he said evenly. "Slowly, just down to your knees."

She turned to see him flexing the pump.

"No, please not that again!" Rather than the slipper, she wanted to feel him, his hand, striking her flesh.

"Very well, but don't expect it to hurt any less."

He didn't strike her at first, but cupped her full but firm buttocks. He patted them just enough to make them jiggle, bouncing the flesh gently in his hand. She could feel the warmth of his caress. The excitement was waning a little, and she was not sure now what she wanted him to do, but with his peremptory: "Six or twelve?" there was no going back. He didn't put her over his knee, but turned her so that she was just in front of him as he sat in the chair. "Stand up straight, and stick your bottom out."

The first blow, for it was harder than a slap, took her breath away, and she felt his hand sink into her behind, leaving its stinging imprint. She didn't cry out, but her intake of breath was deep and sharp. His next spanks were quick, and she knew were designed merely to make her cheeks wobble, he went on well beyond six, and continued the light strokes, teasing, until she felt her whole bottom glowing.

"Ooh!" she cried with a deep intake of breath, and suddenly half a dozen strokes rained down, as hard as she could bear. It hurt more than she had dared believe, but her senses were heightened, and she wanted him to go on.

"More?" he enquired, much more gently now.

"I don't know, it stings, but I, I . . ."

Gently his fingers traced their way round to the front, seeking out her clitoris, finding first the engorged lips, slick with her juices. She was so aroused, and as he slid his fingers up to find the spot, she gasped and pressed against his touch.

"How did you know?" she whispered.

"Know what?" he said.

"That I wanted to be spanked."

"I didn't. Not at first. But I've always fantasized, and I thought . . ."

"Dream come true?" she teased; he ground his finger harder and she gasped again. "Oh I want to come don't make me wait any longer . . . kiss me." She offered her lips hungrily, and he began to kiss her, but after a few moments he drew away.

"What . . . don't stop!"

"If I don't kiss you better . . ." He bent down and gently kissed the cheeks of her bottom, with the occasional little bite. "Lie back," he said.

He turned up the tennis skirt she still wore and pushed her legs apart. He placed his mouth over her pussy and started to tongue her. The exquisite pleasure she felt there was slightly marred by a stinging, flushing sensation that was spreading across her cheeks, pressed as they were against the bed. She tossed and turned. "Take me now!" She wanted to be fucked.

"I still need something to make me really hard," he said reaching down for the slipper. "Since you so thoughtfully brought this with you," he added, flexing it.

"No, just fuck me; really hard. Come on! Now!"

"What a foulmouthed young lady. Over my knee, and we'll teach you some better manners."

"But I want . . ."

"You can't always have what you want, girl. Now do as you're told!"

She wanted the spanking to be over. Her bottom stung now and her pussy ached to be filled. Perhaps if she bent over he'd be quick and then take her. She dutifully bent over his knee, and to her surprise, he eased the full white knickers back up. She raised herself so he could pull them all the way. The feeling of the tight cotton made her aware of her bottom again and the material pulling against her pussy excited her even more.

"Just do something, and quickly! Come on!" she begged desperately. He teased the elastic around the bottom of the knickers, his fingers pushing through to the full plumpness of her cheeks. Gradually he eased the fabric so it bunched into the crack, caressing her all the time. This was exquisite torture for her. Suddenly he pulled the knickers back to cover her fully, and said gruffly, "Count!"

The slipper felt quite different, impersonal, mechanical.

"Aiee!" She couldn't help screaming out as the slaps

rained down. "Stop, stop, you're really hurting!"

"If you think that hurts, try this." And he dropped the gym shoe and spanked her as hard as he could with the flat of his palm. She protested, begging him to stop, but he continued as if possessed. She was almost fainting with the pain, and her bottom was on fire. By now she was sobbing, pleading. Suddenly he stopped, and now she really felt it. The flush of pain engulfed her, awful and exquisite. Not quite the little game she'd had in mind. Confused and hurt she soon felt his arms around her, comforting, caressing. She felt his cock, rock hard against her stomach. She tried not to sob, but the pain was intense. His fingers teased aside the elastic and his hands cupped her buttocks.

"Oh God, fuck me! Fuck me!" The pain now flushed her pussy turning to an unbearable ache. He lay back and she climbed on top of him, tearing down the knickers, grateful that she would bear no weight. She was now so wet that his erection slipped easily home and she rode him gently taking his full length at each stroke. Gradually she quickened her thrusts, enjoying some new-found control over *him*, pushing herself down on to his rock hard prick. He started to pant, "Yes, yes!" He grabbed her bottom pulling her closer; she brushed his hands away wanting to stay in control. She felt him explode deep inside her. Her whole body heaved with the overwhelming sensations that followed and she shuddered in his arms as her orgasm filled her body.

They both subsided on to the bed.

"Christ, I was so turned on," he said.

"Turned on? You were possessed. And yes it bloody well hurts!"

They lay silent for a moment. She turned over. "Still turned on?" she questioned, wiggling slightly.

"Don't you know when to stop . . ?" She couldn't believe she was inviting more punishment.

"You know, the real turn on is starting with a virgin white bottom, so there's no more spanking till you can show me one again."

She eased herself across and, facing down the bed lowered herself trying to stroke his prick with the cleft of her buttocks, aware that he was getting a full view as she moved back and forth. "Better?" she asked, though she had no need to. She could feel him awakening.

"If you move back here a bit . . ." he proffered. And she did so, lowering her pussy within reach of his tongue, and bending down to finish with her lips, the job she had already started. His tongue found her clitoris with practised ease and she couldn't help gyrating her hips slowly enjoying the sensation. By now she was taking the full length of her penis in her mouth.

"Just slow down a second," he whispered, and he left off his delicate lapping, and enjoyed the combination of his, by now, very sensitive prick being gently sucked and the sight and warmth of her well-spanked bottom right before his eyes.

"You're still rather pink, madam, so we'll have to keep this up until your virginal white returns. On the other hand

. . ." But a few more seconds of rapid attention from her had him coming with an intensity he had rarely felt, his semen spurting out hard on to her bosom.

Then just as suddenly she started to orgasm.

"Aah . . . ah . . yes, yes, spank me now; hard as you like, while I'm . . ."

He threw her down and belaboured her now naked and irresistible bottom as she lay flat on the bed. "Yes! Harder! Yes!" she screamed in the grip of waves of powerful orgasm. "Come on, yes, come on."

He couldn't believe she could take it, and slowed his strokes, but with each one there was a gasp and her body was racked with pleasure and pain, and she pushed her buttocks up for more punishment. By now he was rock hard again, and pulling her up, entered her with ease from behind.

At the feel of his prick, she thought she was going to die. "Fill me! Fill me!"

Her passion was so intense, she was insensible to anything around her, so he just hammered on until he came with another overwhelming sensation of pleasure, and she made deep sobbing noises, totally out of control.

They both fell back, exhausted, but satisfied. He caressed her gently, and her sobbing continued. "It really does hurt now, you know." And he cupped her buttocks with the slightest pressure. "I can't believe I really asked for that . . ."

"Another thing you wouldn't believe now," he said quietly, "is that you will ask me to do it all again some-

BETTINA AND CANDY

time soon." And even as she was about to protest, she felt a stirring deep inside at the mere suggestion.

Bettina writes,

No one likes being taken for a ride . . . do they?

Riding a Jaguar

RIDING A JAGUAR

Rivulets of water ran down her body, cascading to the floor as Angie stepped from the shower. The fluffy towel briefly caressed her wet skin before being discarded. Her hand reached for the razor. The blades deliciously grazed against her soft, damp pussy, her auburn curls falling to the floor. She returned the razor to its box and sprayed perfume across her body in a gentle mist.

It was a warm summer morning. The sheer voile curtains were billowing out against the breeze. Angie enjoyed the feeling of the warm air on her skin as she turned to view herself in the mirror. Her thick auburn hair shone in the sunlight and her breasts were still firm and supple. Her tummy was flat and her legs were long and slim. She remembered when Martin couldn't leave her alone. She paused to touch herself, sliding a finger around her pussy lips; it had been months since she'd felt a man between her legs.

Today she was planning a surprise for her husband. They had drifted so far apart and she desperately wanted him to desire her again. Walking to the bed she picked up the underwear she had laid out before her shower. Putting it on, she revelled in the feel of silk stockings sliding over her legs. A transparent g-string highlighted her freshly shorn pussy, and the thong nestled tightly between her buttocks. She wanted Martin inside her, to feel his hard cock pushing its way into her cunt. Reaching into the lingerie drawer, she found her companion. It lay hidden beneath layers of silk. Her fingers making contact she paused to stroke it before pulling it out into the light. She pressed the on-button and eight inches of sheer pleasure began to pulsate. Pulling the g-string down, kicking it across the floor, Angie lay on the bed. Parting her legs she rubbed the vibrator over her pussy lips then slowly she brought it up to buzz against her clitoris before moving it back down again. Her juices flowing, milky white cum was travelling down the black rubber and over her red fingernails to soak into the cotton bed linen. Angie arched her back, her breathing turned into short gasps. The sensations from the vibrator were electrifying her, and she opened her legs wider. She began writhing on the sheets as the vibrator was whipping up and down her slit. The desire to be filled was overwhelming. Seeing herself in the bedroom mirror, the eroticism of watching her sexual responses intensified her pleasure. The mirror was reflecting her pussy, oozing cum. Stimulating her hard erect nipples with her free hand, she felt her pussy pulsing harder against the rubber. Fantasizing, she imagined her mouth filled with a grateful cock, another one pumping her aching pussy. Climbing to orgasm both her hands gripped the vibrator as she rammed it in and out.

She lay gasping for some minutes, too weak even to pull the vibrator out. Running her fingers through her hair she couldn't believe she'd been that horny.

Eventually she made her way to the bathroom and showered her pussy. Stretched and swollen the cold water was calming. Patting herself gently dry, she decided not to tidy up. Walking through the bedroom she saw the vibrator discarded on the crumpled sheets. Grinning cheekily, she hoped Martin would use it on her cunt later.

In the hallway she stopped to ease her feet into a pair of high heeled sandals. Naked apart from her stockings, she slipped on a short mac and hurried to the car.

Feeling vibrant and alive she slid into her Mercedes. Trembling with anticipation she swung her beautiful car out of the driveway. Despite it being early, the heat was already starting to build and the atmosphere inside the car was stifling. A prickly sweat broke out over her body, but she didn't switch on the air conditioning; she wanted to greet Martin with beads of sweat glistening on her breasts.

Martin ran his own company not far from home. Within fifteen minutes she was there. Feeling every beat of her heart she reached the rear entrance and opened the door. She hurried down the corridor to his office, hoping that no one would see her. Slowly, silently she turned the handle of the door. The reception room was empty. Angie crept inside and closed the door behind her. Everything was going to plan. The door was slightly open and she could hear noises from inside. She peeked through the open crack. Freezing, she was unable to believe her eyes. She saw Martin's secretary sprawled across his desk. Martin, sweating profusely, was heaving himself into her.

"Gloria, you're the only woman I can get this hard for. This is all for you my beautiful baby," he grunted.

Gloria ceased massaging her huge tits. "Oh Martin, you're such a man. So big . . . so hard . . . so oh!" she gasped.

"Get down in front of me," Martin demanded as he pulled his dick out of her cunt.

Squatting before him, Gloria lifted her breasts, "Oh come on baby, give it to me. Show me what that big cock can do," she gushed.

Rubbing frantically at his penis he thrust it towards her. "You gorgeous little whore. . ." His ejaculation exploded across her breasts. His creamy cum spilling down on to her stomach.

"Ooh, you naughty boy! You love that don't you, spurting your spunk all over my tits. Now, come to mummy baby, come here and lick me out," she begged.

Angie couldn't stand it anymore. Turning on her heels she left the building and ran to the car. Tears of pain coursed down her cheeks, her world destroyed.

It was with disdain that she eyed Martin the following morning. Watching him snore, his pot belly quivering. She now realised everything about him made her feel sick. Lying flat on his back, mouth wide open, he resembled an optimistic fly trap. Feeling the venom rise, she leaned over and grabbed his flaccid penis.

"What the fuck do you think you're doing?" he bellowed, waking with a violent start.

"Just testing for life."

"You fucking bitch! Let go of it," he yelled.

She was in no mood to let go. "Saving it for Gloria, are you? You bastard!"

"What's she done? Why are you having a go at her?"

"I saw you two yesterday. It was revolting! What the hell did you think you were doing?" Angie demanded, releasing his cock in disgust.

"Fucking actually. Why? Are you jealous?" he said mockingly.

"How could you touch that little slut? What a whore she is. She'd fuck anything."

"Well at least she doesn't nag all the time like you do. At least she knows when to keep her mouth shut."

"You mean when it isn't full of your cock." Angie sat on the edge of the bed. "How could you do this to me," she said, her voice cracking with emotion.

Martin walked to the dressing table. "You don't want me anymore, you just want the money," he said bitterly.

Tears streamed down Angie's face. "It's not true, it's just not true!" she exclaimed.

Martin took the vibrator out of the drawer and tossed it on to the bed. "Is this what you use for a man these days?" he said sarcastically.

"You bastard! You great fat fucking bastard," she screamed. Picking up the vibrator she threw it at him.

"I'll find myself a man. Two can play at this game."

"Oh no you won't, you're past it now," Martin mocked.

BETTINA AND CANDY

Fleeing the house she ran to her car. Getting in she felt stupid and old. Starting the car she sped away. She forced herself to stop crying and telling herself he wasn't worth it she pulled herself together.

Not sure of where she was going she drove around aimlessly. She just knew that she'd had it with playing the perfect wife.

Pulling up behind a Jaguar at traffic lights, she remembered James. Blonde, young and beautiful, he worked at the Jaguar dealership. Angie had met him when Martin wanted to change his car. He'd decided on a Jaguar and she'd put it down to his mid-life crisis. She remembered her visit to the dealership. One morning, despite her protests, Martin had insisted on driving there. After locating a salesman he'd launched himself with vitriolic gusto into heated negotiations. Beady eyed with boredom and unable to stifle her yawns any longer, she'd decided to take a stroll around the forecourt. Lost in thought and idly tracing her finger across the bonnet of automotive perfection, she'd heard a soft, deep voice.

"Beautiful isn't it?"

She nearly jumped out of her skin.

"Sorry did I startle you?" The voice belonged to a gorgeous young man. Long and lean limbed he reached at least six foot tall. Soft blonde hair framed a perfectly proportioned face. Behind his deep blue eyes she saw the irresistible combination of boyish vulnerability mixed with smouldering sexuality.

"I didn't hear you behind me, that's all," she'd replied, taking a deep breath.

"My name is James, can I help you with anything?" he asked quietly.

"Oh no thank you I'm here with my husband, he's with one of your colleagues. I find it all very boring. I can't understand what you men find so fascinating, a car is just a car isn't it?"

"No, well I'll admit some cars are just functional, but the cars in our showroom are more than that, they are beautiful. When you drive one, it's as if you've got a beautiful woman on your arm, and you're showing her off in a really posh restaurant. I can see that your husband has excellent taste in cars *and* women."

Angie had felt herself blush at his words. This gorgeous young man was flirting with her. She felt her nipples harden and push against the thin fabric of her dress. "So a car is just an extension of a man's penis," she couldn't believe she had said that.

"Oh yes and as with a penis it's how you drive it that counts. If you ever want me to take you for a test drive, just pop in and I'd be very happy to take you for a spin."

"I'll keep that in mind," she'd replied. Not daring to meet his eyes again she turned and walked away. As she had crossed the showroom she'd caught sight of herself in a mirror. Her nipples were showing clearly under her dress and James' eyes were fixed on her arse.

Since that day he'd plagued her thoughts, but she'd kept putting him out of her mind, concentrating on her husband. She'd been trying to make it work with Martin.

Now she didn't give a damn. With determination she hit the accelerator and directed her car towards the dealership marked 'Jaguar'.

Even the power of the engine as she accelerated reminded her a man's power as he thrust into her. Everywhere she looked there was sex, everything reminded her of sex, so why wasn't she getting any.

Feeling apprehensive she realised she was approaching the dealership and she began to have doubts. Had she misread the situation? Was she going to make a fool of herself? She pulled onto the forecourt, removed the ignition keys and took a moment to compose herself. She checked her lipstick in the mirror, her lip line was perfect, and her gloss red lipstick thickly covered her full lips. With her hands she adjusted her bosoms, making full use of her cleavage.

James appeared, freshly shaven and smelling delicious. She wanted to reach out and touch him, she had never felt this horny before.

"Hello Mrs Hughes how are you today?" he asked. Angie couldn't take her eyes off him. It was terribly hot and she felt flustered.

"I just thought I'd call in as I was passing, I want to take another look at that XKR," she answered. Angie wanted to taste his sensuous lips, to take his cock in her mouth, to mark it with her lipstick.

"Shall we take the car out for a test drive?" he asked. Her tummy lurched as she saw the desire in his eyes. Feeling her nipples stiffen and her pussy throb, she struggled to deliver a calm and confident, "Yes please."

The car stood in pride of place on the front forecourt. Red and majestic it possessed a beautiful predatory readiness. Angie followed him towards it, beneath his trousers his buttocks looked firm, she imagined what it would be like to grip them while he fucked her. Reaching the car he opened the driver's door for her, and she got in. Despite her excitement, the sheer beauty of the car still took her aback. She was seeing cars in a new light, they were about sex and glamour. . . and fucking.

"It's absolutely gorgeous," she gasped.

James then turned his full gaze on her, "Sir William Lyons once said of his beloved Jaguars that the product itself had always been designed to give its owner pleasure."

Angie shifted in her seat. She was soaking. Gripping the leather steering wheel she noticed how it softened to leave indents of her fingers. Would his young flesh yield so easily. She was trembling so much it took her three goes to start the car. Eventually she was able to ease it off the forecourt. They headed out of town.

The car ate the miles with ease, and it wasn't long before they reached the open road. Sweat was trickling down her back and between her breasts but James had made no effort to switch the air conditioning on. Nothing had been said since they had left the showroom. Had she misjudged James? Perhaps he wasn't interested in sex with her, perhaps he just wanted to make a sale.

It was James who broke the silence, "I hope you don't

mind me saying Mrs Hughes, but I have to tell you, you look lovely in that dress, the colour really suits you."

She blushed. Was he making a move? "Oh thank you, it's silk," she stammered.

"So I see," he replied, brushing his hand across her thigh. She felt as if electricity was running through her. His hand remained on her thigh. Did he want her? There was only one way to find out. Gradually she eased her legs apart. He needed no further cue, immediately his hand slipped under her dress and made its way up her leg, until he was touching the bottom of her knickers. She opened her legs a little wider and his fingers found her clitoris through her thin cotton panties.

"Ooh yes," she panted, "I want you to fuck me, perhaps we could find somewhere to stop?"

"Take the track approaching on your left," said James hurriedly. Spotting it, she swung the car hard left. Stones and dirt ricocheted past the windows as it cannoned across the hard tyre tracks. Angie put the brakes on and they came to a stop.

Immediately James turned, kissing her full on the lips. His tongue exploring her mouth, his hands were all over her breasts. Pulling away they released their seat belts.

"Follow me," he said.

Getting out, following him to the front of the car, she raised her dress. James lifted her onto the bonnet, pulling at her panties, ripping them in his urgency. Unzipping his trousers, Angie saw how massive he was. She'd never seen such a big cock. Enthusiastically she cupped and stroked his heavy balls, twitching and oozing pre-cum his penis was ready. Feeling as if she was going to explode, her wetness sizzled on the hot bonnet. She was desperate for his hard cock.

"Fuck me James, fuck me . . . please, put it in, do it now!" she cried. With that, James grasped her soft buttocks and thrust hard into her. She gasped with shock, she'd never had a man so big before. His penis had stretched her until she was completely full. James stroked her slowly with his cock. "I've wanted to take you since the day you walked into the showroom. You're so fucking beautiful," he panted as he thrust harder into her.

"I wanted you too James," she replied.

Angie pushed against him matching him stroke for stroke. The anticipation had been to much for her she could feel herself beginning to climax. She pushed a hand between her legs and found her clitoris. "Ooh James I can't go on I'm coming. . . ooh!" she screamed as her climax ripped through her.

James pulled himself out, he was smothered in her cum. He pulled her down to meet him. Pushing her pert breasts together he slid his rigid cock between them. He thrust twice and let go, hot semen spurted out, covering her breasts in his creamy spunk. She put her fingers in it and licked them with relish. Laughing she said. "You taste as good as you look."

"Can I suggest the back seat for a little more comfort?"

Angie slid off the bonnet and followed him. Naked

apart from her high heels, she rubbed his cum into her breasts flicking her nipples back and forth.

It had been so long since she'd had a young body that she'd forgotten how quickly they recover. His penis was already stiffening. She spread herself across the back seat, her legs parted, her cunt wide open. She delighted in being so wanton and enjoyed feeling him upon her once more. The warmth of James's body softened her nipples and she was content to lay in his arms as he had her again. The car gently rocked on its suspension. Then her desire to climax took over. Angie lifted her hips and pushed hard against him. James responded, fucking her hard with every thrust. Feeling his cock so far up inside her intensified the sensation. Frantically rubbing her breasts she was desperate for another orgasm. Bending his head, James took her nipple into his mouth. Sucking on it brought her to the brink.

"I'm going to come!" she gasped.

Pulling back James gave her the full length of his cock. Stretching her cunt to the limit.

"Wait, I want to go on top," she blurted out. Changing positions, Angie straddled him, forcing herself down hard on to his cock, then pulling herself up its full length. Writhing her pussy up and down, twisting to increase the friction, she pumped down on him before letting go. Screaming she arched her back as her orgasm gushed over his scrotum. Dazed and disorientated it took her a moment to realise he was tensing.

"I'm exploding!" he shouted. She leaned back as he

raised his hips. Long, hot bursts ejaculated up high inside her.

Afterwards they lay in each other's arms. James was the first to speak. "It's time we were getting back, the car's had a good work out."

"Do we have to? I'm only just getting warmed up," she giggled.

"Come on, I'll help you get dressed. I'm afraid you'll have to do without your knickers though," he said. "Your shaved pussy really got me going," he laughed. Remembering whom she had shaved it for she refused to feel guilty.

"You'll have to drive, I need a blow dry," she joked. Slipping her dress back on and clambering into the front of the car Angie felt sad that it was nearly over. Sitting in the passenger seat, her legs spread open, she was drying her knickerless pussy in the stream of cool air from the air vent. Disappointed to see the showroom looming, she said softly, "I've had a wonderful time James."

"The pleasure was all mine," he said. Pulling on to the forecourt he parked the car and applied the handbrake. She got out and watched James as he leaned against the Jaguar. Admiring their collective beauty, she was lost in thought, until the voice of one of his colleagues interrupted.

"Good morning Mrs Hughes, nice to see you again." It was Mike, another salesman. "What did you think of the car?" he asked. She wished he would piss off.

"Well I have to say that I was very impressed, its performance is truly outstanding," she said, smiling.

"Perhaps James could show you some options. I'll leave you in his capable hands then."

"Perhaps I should. Please follow me to the office Mrs Hughes," James said.

Angie followed James across the tarmac. He held the office door open for her and she entered. Walking to the table she leaned over and started to leaf through the glossy brochures. James moved up behind her. The pictures of the Jaguars blurred as Angie felt his hand slide up her leg, simultaneously lifting her dress and undoing his zipper. Quivering with excitement she raised her bottom in anticipation. She couldn't believe it, being taken again so soon. Pulling her legs apart his penis slid in.

"Fuck me James, fuck me hard," she begged.

Gripping her tight he started to pump. Reaching for her clit, lost in pure pleasure, she fingered it. He thrust deeper and harder. Pushing her bottom out, she enjoyed every inch he was giving her. Writhing on his cock sent Angie into a frenzy.

"Harder, deeper, fuck my cunt!" she demanded.

"Whatever the customer wants the customer gets," he gasped.

Pulling away she broke from his grasp, turning to look at him she said, "Come here . . . you are so gorgeous." He was standing before her, his cock erect and quivering, and she dropped to her knees.

"Put it in," she ordered.

Her wide open mouth was too much, he started to come. She took him in her mouth just in time. Grasping her hair, pulling her hard towards him Angie had his whole length inside her mouth. Stroking her clit in time to his satisfying thrusts, she received hot, salty cum straight down her throat. James released her. Taught and shaking, Angie spread herself on the floor. Opening her legs wide she inserted two fingers and stretched her pussy lips wide open. Recovering, James went down on her and buried his blonde hair in her throbbing pussy. He licked her sex lips, tasting her juices. He teased her clit with his tongue, Angie played with her breasts, rubbing her nipples between her thumb and forefinger until they were hard and erect. James' tongue probed her sex, her pussy was soaking. Arching her back she tensed, " Ooh, lick me, lick my clit, ooh I'm coming... now!" She came, again and again in long shuddering waves.

It was a while before she could speak, they both lay totally spent.

"I think the XKR will be too much of a handful for my husband can I try something else?" Angie smiled.

"Of course, customer satisfaction has always been my priority," James replied, pushing his fringe back he kissed her gently.

Bettina writes,

I stay in a lot of hotels and I know from experience that often the laundry service leaves a lot to be desired. The lady in this story however, gets some really good service . . .

Coming Clean

COMING CLEAN

The basque tumbled out from between the piles of bedclothes and fell at Paul's feet. He stared at it for a long moment. There was no one else in the laundry just then. Against the expensive, chaste crispness of the finest Irish linen, the red and black lace looked even more provocative. He bent to pick it up. The very stiffness of the lace made the skin on his fingertips tingle. He wondered which of the outwardly respectable hotel guests had last flaunted this between the sheets - those same sheets it was his job to sort and load into the machines. She must be beautiful, he thought. As he handled the white cotton, he imagined her half-naked body writhing against it as he touched her all over and brought her to orgasm. Lovingly he turned the wispy garment over in his hands. It laced up with black satin ribbon all down the front. The detail was purely nonfunctional, of course, as it had the normal hook and eye fastening at the back. Yes, this arrangement, he was delighted to discover, was purely for titillation. He could just imagine slowly unthreading the narrow black satin, and watching the stiff lace panels part under the heaviness of the ample white breasts that were sliding into his hands.

Paul's cock was stirring with the beginnings of an erection. It put the cherry on top of the cake to look inside the label - 36DD it read. The fantasy cup size. And how those breasts would feel in his hands, firm and soft and round. Paul felt the front of his trousers tighten even more. The supervisor could be back any minute now. Paul didn't want him to see the basque. He didn't want to have to hand it back. He felt as possessive as a lover. He knew what to do. He'd hide it in the filing cabinet drawer where the linen records were kept. He was the only person likely to look in there over the next few hours. Tonight, he'd take it home to his bedsit and bury his face in it, pretending he was lost in the pillow of those yielding breasts, and his own hand would bring him to a bursting orgasm. He pressed his nose and mouth against the basque to give himself a foretaste. It was sweet and musky with the scent of a woman's sex . . .

Suddenly there were footsteps in the corridor; the supervisor must be coming back. Paul hurriedly shoved the precious basque into the cabinet drawer, and snatched a pile of laundry into his lap to hide the significant bulge at his crotch. He pretended to be busy.

"Excuse me."

Paul looked up. That wasn't a familiar voice. In the doorway of the laundry room stood a stunning woman. She must have been in her mid-thirties, draped in an expensive cashmere coat, and luxuriant chestnut hair lapped her shoulders. Her shapely legs were coated in sheer black nylon that whispered tantalizingly, thigh against thigh, as she walked very slowly into the room.

"I seem to have lost something," she said. "I wonder if you can help me?"

"I - I hope so," Paul stammered. Please, no, he thought, it couldn't be. To find such a perfect masturbatory fantasy object, only to have it snatched away moments later, was just too cruel.

"What have you mislaid madam? Maybe I can help you."

The woman lowered her eyes. "A certain . . . item of underwear. Red and black. I can't think where else it could be. It must have got bundled up with my sheets after last night." She raised her eyes to meet Paul's again. "Let's just say I'm sure you'd know it if you saw it."

The dilemma tightened Paul's stomach. He didn't want to lie, but the thought of relinquishing that basque . . .

"My, it's warm in here," she breathed, while Paul was still trying to find the words to answer her. "However do you manage to work in this heat?" She slipped the coat from her shoulders. Beneath it was an equally expensive black jersey dress. It moulded itself to her curvy body. Paul's gaze went straight to her breasts and stayed there. 36DD the label had said. Well, he didn't doubt that she filled out those cups magnificently. As she moved nonchalantly around the room her fingertips trailed from her neck down to her cleavage and back again. She paused with her body in profile to Paul's. The black curve of her prominent bosom was silhouetted against the piles and piles of white sheets. She must surely know what sort of effect she was having on him.

"I hope you can find it," she murmured, and then turned conspiratorially to face him. "I really, really need it for tonight. I'm going to one of those fancy dinner dances and I want to wear a strapless dress. I don't think I ought to risk it without my basque."

As if to make her point she wriggled her shoulders a little. Paul's stare was caught like a rabbit's, as her breasts jiggled under her dress. He took a deep breath and closed his eyes momentarily. Yes, he could understand all too well. He imagined that deep, velvety cleavage in a low cut strapless evening gown. He imagined the woman before him leaning over towards her dinner companion to catch something he'd said, allowing another inch of those generous breasts to slide out from beneath the taffeta to meet him. Paul's cock was rock hard and pressing against his fly insistently.

When he opened his eyes the mystery woman was standing closer to him. Her own gaze was lowered again. He didn't buy into this coyness for a minute. A ripe, experienced woman like her, she must know full well what the power of her body language was doing to a young man of twenty-one.

"I'll certainly do my best to find it for you," Paul said reluctantly. "In fact, if you'd like to wait here a moment, I'll see . . ." He slid the drawer open a couple of inches. Edging the fingers inside they made contact with the wispy lace. Amazing to think that something so flimsy could keep such a magnificent pair of breasts in check. God, she must be firm to get away with it. He longed to know.

His skin tingled with the touch of the lace. Giving it up was agony, but now he'd met her in the flesh, the fantasy of her wearing it was some compensation.

"Don't worry now," she said, holding up her hand. "I've got to go out, I can't hang around. But I'll be back just after lunch. Please, if you wouldn't mind, you could bring it up to my room then . . . if you manage to find it of course. I'm in room 143."

"Yes I will. I promise. I'll look for it right away."

"You're very kind."

She smiled and leaned forward a little to check his name badge. He felt her hot breath on his neck, and her perfume was sweet and inticing.

"Thank you so much . . . Paul. I was told how helpful the staff were at The Western Star. That's why I chose it."

And then the cashmere coat was slung over one shoulder, and the sheer black nylon stockings swished they way towards the door.

"I'm sorry," Paul called after her. "What did you say your name was?"

"Mrs Kinsella," she replied without turning.

The burning in his groin turned instantly to an iciness just beneath his solar plexus. *She* was Mrs Kinsella. There were rumours about Mrs Kinsella. Everyone you spoke to in the tourist industry had heard her name. She was thought to be an undercover reviewer for a very upmarket hotel guide. And he'd spent the whole time ogling her breasts as if he'd never seen a pair before! A coldness crept down the back of his neck. He'd been set up. He imagined sexual harassment accusations and waving goodbye to his job.

At half past one Paul tentatively knocked at the door of room 143. The basque was wrapped in tissue paper, clutched in his hands. He hoped his palms weren't sweating too much. His mouth, by contrast, was completely dry. He'd act the professional. He'd be helpful but polite, and at all costs keep his gaze above her neckline, though God knows that wasn't going to be easy. Then she might forgive his earlier leering and he might just keep his job.

"Come in, it isn't locked."

Paul couldn't see anyone at first as he entered the room. Mrs Kinsella appeared at the door of the en suite bathroom. Paul's resolution about keeping eye contact dropped along with his jaw. She was wearing a scarlet silk kimono that was only just long enough to keep him guessing as to whether she was wearing panties or not. Her stocking tops peeped out from beneath the silk and as she walked across the room towards him, the sheer black nylon swished again as inner thigh rubbed inner thigh. Until that moment Paul wouldn't have believed it was possible to get turned on just by a sound.

"Oh you angel! You found it!" she said, looking down at the tissue paper packet in his hands. "You didn't have to gift wrap it though!"

"Can you imagine the looks I'd have got if I hadn't? Walking through the hotel foyer with a woman's sexy lingerie in my hand."

She smiled. "Point taken."

The thought of her bending over with no panties filled his mind, and he couldn't stop the images coming of the silk rising over her bare arse and her pussy coming into view. She reached out and took the packet from Paul's hands. He resisted ever so slightly before letting go. It was covering the front of his trousers and his erection wasn't easy to disguise.

"It was so sweet of you to bring it back to me," she purred. "But, wouldn't you just know it, when I was out shopping this lunchtime, I saw another basque. Even naughtier. I know it's wicked of me but I just couldn't resist it. What d'you think?"

She undid the belt of her silky kimono and let it fall open. Paul inhaled sharply. She looked breathtaking in the sheer black basque. She had no panties on and her small wispy triangle of pubic hair was still moist from her shower. The basque encased her body. The tight squeeze of the see-through cups made the exposed upper curves of her breasts outrageously round. She was bound but at the same time deliciously on display. Paul edged back involuntarily towards the door.

"Mrs Kinsella, I . . ."

"Paul, really, I think you ought to start calling me Lydia." She took a deep breath and the effect in that particular outfit was incredible. The basque design was almost the same as the one Paul had returned, but the panels of this one were made of something black, glossy, and every bit as translucent as her stockings. As she inhaled, the large dark circles of her nipples crushed themselves even more forcefully against their see-through prison. It moulded itself to her voluptuous body like no other fabric he had seen.

"What do you think?" she demanded.

"I think you're putting me in an impossible situation, Mrs Kinsella. I mean . . my job . ."

"No, what d'you think about the basque? Does it turn you on?"

"No . . of course not madam," Paul lied, trying to keep himself out of trouble.

She looped the belt of her kimono around the back of his neck and drew him close to her. She pressed her lips to his and kissed him fully and deeply. Her hand glided down the front of his trousers. She sighed appreciatively as she fondled the outline of his bulging cock.

"I've got someone here who thinks it's a turn on," she whispered. "I bet if I took him in my mouth and sucked him off, he'd come like champagne all over me. And five minutes later he'd be standing to attention again, and ready to fuck me out of my mind."

Paul bit his lip. The images her words were creating in his head came perilously close to making it all come true. Surely, he thought, she'd gone too far for this to be a test of his professionalism as a member of the hotel staff. It seemed she was more interested in a good time. He decided that either way he'd surrender to the inevitable.

"The staff at The Western Star aim to please their

guests at all times," he said. "Whatever I can do to please you madam . . ."

She smiled. "So come here and please me then." She took a firm hold of the scarlet kimono belt that was still looped around his neck and led him to the enormous double bed. He let her take the lead as it seemed to really turn her on. She undid the buttons of his shirt, deliberately, slowly, and grazed her perfectly shaped nails over the scattering of hairs on his chest. She followed the hair when it became a thin dark line heading down across his stomach and beyond. With an obviously practised dexterity, she undid the belt of his trousers with her teeth and eased down the zip. Her long fingers unhooked the waistband of his briefs from the tip of his straining erection to set it free. Her breath caressing the length of his shaft was torture.

"I love sucking a young eager cock," she murmured. "Ooh it's so hard too!" Her mouth gently pressed against the tip of Paul's erection in small kisses. "I must take it in my mouth." More little kisses followed, and her teasing had Paul's huge, hard cock stretching to get inside her mouth. She ran her tongue along the hardness of his shaft from its base to its tip and back again.

"You taste so good," she whispered, "I can't wait to suck you dry." Lydia took the base of Paul's cock in her hands. Then she parted her soft red lips, and gazed up into his eyes as her hot wet mouth engulfed his throbbing penis, sucking it down to the back of her throat. She sucked hard and long and Paul thought he wasn't going to be able to hold back from coming. Then she became more gentle and slow. The very tip of her tongue flicked the head of his cock, and then traced the line to and fro along the sensitive underside of his penis. Paul wondered how many other men she'd taken into that exquisite mouth to get this good. The thought of her sucking off so many men turned him on even more. Her nails lightly brushed the hairs on his scrotum, and he could feel the skin moving as it pulled his balls tight against his body. One of her inquisitive fingertips wriggled further back and began to circle the delicate skin of his anus. Paul didn't even have time to be shocked, the sensation was mind-blowing. But just as he felt the blood surging through his already bursting penis for that explosive climax, she pulled away from him. With a slow smile that reminded him she liked being in charge, Lydia raised herself up until her thrusting breasts were level with his face.

"Set them free," she told him, "you know it's been what you've been wanting to do since you first laid eyes on them."

Half way down her velvety cleavage nestled a satin bow. Paul tugged at one end. It glided apart, and tension released, the curiously yielding panels of the basque began to move. He couldn't wait to assist the process. Fingers trembling, he began to unthread the narrow ribbon from its eyelets. Just as the huge dark circles of her nipples were rising like suns above their translucent cups she put her hand over his.

"Stop there," she said. "I want to see myself being

unwrapped." Lydia swung herself off the bed and walked decisively over to the Victorian dressing table in the corner of the room.

"Come here!" she ordered. Paul did as he was told, somewhat self-consciously, as his frustrated erection swayed to and fro before him, as he hurried over to join her.

"Stand behind me," she continued. "Now .. carry on with what you were doing."

Paul rested the tip of his swollen cock just above the cleft of her bare arse, between the two beguiling dimples at the base of her spine. He reached round and began unlacing the front of her basque once more. There was something so decadent about watching it all happening in the antique mirror. Her firm breasts spilled out into his hands, white as two full moons. Free from their restraints, her nipples instantly peaked. From the rapt look on Lydia's face, Paul could tell this exposure of her own voluptuous body was turning her on unbearably. She gazed into the mirror and leaned forward a little. It set her breasts swinging invitingly. She grasped the back of the high Victorian chair and tilted her arse towards Paul like a bitch on heat.

"You see that crop down there?" she snapped. "Pick it up and use it on me. I'm sure I don't have to tell you how."

He saw the fine leather riding crop propped against the antique dressing table. Truth was he'd noticed it before but just assumed, well, The Western Star was on the edge of pony-trekking country and some guests liked a canter on the moors. Lydia Kinsella obviously preferred more unusual past-times.

Paul picked up the riding crop and tested it once against the flat of his hand. He looked down at the bare backside Lydia was presenting for him. He let his fingers trail across its mounds and she quivered under his touch. He ran the tip of the crop upwards along the outside of her stockinged thigh and come to rest on her back.

"Now! Do it now!" Lydia ordered impatiently.

Paul wasn't at all sure he would give her what she wanted just yet. For the first time he was in charge, and he was going to make the most of it. He touched the length of the crop gently against her soft white cheeks, and pressed its hardness into her flesh for a moment. Then he took it away, to bring it back again for another light touch. His preparations were proving too much for Lydia.

"Now, please, please do it now . . ." she begged.

"Oh, I'm sorry madam I didn't realise. Would you like it now?"

"Yes - please!" Lydia answered in desperation.

He drew back his hand and smacked the crop down against her arse. She cried out loud. He brought it down across her pale, white, buttocks, this way and that, again and again. Again she cried out. Lydia Kinsella, the powerful hotel reviewer was having her arse whipped scarlet by a mere laundry boy and she was loving every minute of it. He watched her face in the mirror. The rapture that fell across it as he brought the crop down against her flesh was sending his cock wild to get it inside her cunt. When the pert cheeks of her buttocks were positively glowing Paul ceased his strokes.

"Fuck me from behind," she cried. "Now!"

Paul wasn't about to argue, he stroked the warm cheeks of her arse, pulling them as far apart as they would go. He trailed the moist tip of his penis along the stretched skin between them. For a moment he paused by the puckering ring of her anus and teased it with his cock. In the mirror he read the thrill in her eyes as his erection pressed there. She was wondering, hoping even, that he was about to sink his shaft deep in her arse. Then he smiled, pressed on, and found the succulent tenderness of her sex. He parted her pussy lips with two probing fingertips and thrust his cock in deep. It was so satisfying to hear her gasp. She was tighter than he ever would have imagined but so, so, wet. He clenched his buttocks and drove into her again; his thrusts were long and smooth and he raised his hands back to her luscious breasts. He pinched each nipple between thumb and forefinger and teased them. Tiny involuntary sounds began coming from Lydia's throat. He squeezed her nipples harder, this time showing no mercy. Her moans of ecstasy grew louder still. It excited him to thrill her and control her pleasure. With his hard young cock inside her she was completely given over to carnal lust. It was his cock, his skills that were doing this to her. Of all the lovers Lydia must have had before, it was he, Paul, giving her the most pleasure. He was sure there was no way she could be acting. He pumped faster and her vaginal muscles clasped against his thrusting shaft. Paul groaned and shuddered with the extra stimulation. He knew he couldn't hold back his ejaculation much longer. He pinched the very tips of her nipples and rolled them in his fingertips. This sent her wild, and she was coming - thank God - she was coming. The pitch of her cries couldn't mean anything else. The sight of her in the mirror enjoying herself so much through his skill brought Paul to the very brink of his explosive climax. Paul's thrusts were fast and savage now and he felt the tension mount in his balls, the muscles contract at the base of his cock, and then the surge of sweet satisfaction as his spunk spurted inside her.

The next edition of the exclusive hotel guide was published that spring. The Western Star got an excellent review. There was even a quirky footnote concerning the obliging nature of the laundry staff. Later that year, Paul received a promotion, and then a transfer to the company's flagship London hotel. By the age of twenty-five he was manager of domestic services there.

It happened on a balmy day in late summer. He was making his way down to check the laundry staff rota when, behind the half-closed door, he heard a voice which made his heart beat a little faster.

"Excuse me, I was wondering . . . could you help me? I seem to have lost a certain item of underwear. I can only think it got mixed up with my sheets . . ."

Paul peered through the crack between the door and

the door frame. Lydia was wearing a thin cotton summer dress that clung provocatively to her magnificent curves. Her breasts were still as firm and thrusting as he remembered them. Her flimsy dress moved tantalisingly as she shifted her weight from one leg to the other, wiggling her backside. He looked at that beautiful arse and remembered it offered up bare for him to whip.

As Lydia turned and left the room, Paul hid behind one of the tall linen trolleys. He waited until her stiletto-heeled footsteps faded down the corridor, and then he went into the laundry room. Tom the laundry boy was busy unloading the sheets.

"Have you found what the lady was looking for Tom?"

"No, I haven't sir."

"I'll help you look for it. I've got the feeling it's here somewhere."

Paul and Tom began to look through the baskets of linen, and as they pulled out some of the white sheets, a sexy black basque fell out on to the floor.

Paul smiled to himself.

"I'll deal with this Tom," he said, scooping up the evidence. Mrs Kinsella was a very naughty girl. And he was going to give her every chance to confess . . . with a little encouragement.

Bettina writes,

The girl in this story is a good friend of mine. Name changed for obvious reasons - she wouldn't want her husband to find out!

She told me about this adventure as soon as she got back from America. She says it was a one-off, and now that she's got it out of her system, it won't happen again . . . but somehow I don't believe her.

Candy:

I know what you mean Bettina, you can't just do it one time, can you? Not once you've got the taste for it!

The Angel Room

THE ANGEL ROOM

'Ladies, have you ever wondered what it would be like . .' the advert read. I kept reading that same ad over and over. Yes, of course I'd wondered what it would be like. And just lately I had been seriously thinking of doing something about it. Especially since I'd been staying in New York. Everyone was so much more up-front than in England. If I was going to try it, this was the place.

My hotel was only a few blocks away from 42nd Street, and I often walked there to look in the sex shops, and watch the sexy girls ply their trade on the street. I had to admit some of them did look lovely. I often fantasized about sex with them, but they looked so brash that I didn't have the courage to approach them. I didn't know what they'd think, having a woman ask for sex, and what their response might be. I looked at the advert again. It read:

'Ladies, have you ever wondered what it would be like to feel the touch of another woman? An intimate service to satisfy all your desires. Visit The Angel Room.'

It sounded like my perfect opportunity to set aside my reservations, and go for it. After all, you only live once. No one at home would ever find out, the big advantage of doing it in another country. And when I go back home it will all be a thing of the past and my husband

Ladies . . .
have you ever wondered what it would be like to feel the touch of another woman?

We offer a discreet
and intimate service
to satisfy all
your desires

Visit The Angel Room

need never know. He wouldn't like it, and I would never want to hurt his feelings. It's not that our two years of marriage hadn't been happy, but I could never be fulfilled without knowing how it felt to be with a woman. To feel another woman's lips touch mine, to feel another woman's passion.

I tentatively dialled the number. It was answered by a woman's voice.

"Hello, this is The Angel Room, Emma speaking, how may I help you?"

I took a deep breath . . .

"I saw your advert. I was wondering if you could tell me something about your services?"

"Yes, certainly madam. The Angel Room is a place for women to come and fulfill their desires. No men are allowed as the service is for women only. We have eight lovely girls who dedicate themselves to pleasing women. The atmosphere is friendly and relaxed and you are most welcome to come and have a look around if you wish, with no obligation. Once you are here, if you feel you'd like to go ahead and enjoy the attention of any of our girls you can do so. Would you like to come down and have a look around?"

"How much do you charge?"

"Well, we charge by time, so there is no hidden extras. This also means there's no interruption to your enjoyment with the girls, and they will never say to you 'Oh, that will be extra'. You can be confident of the price I give you. Prices start at $200, and that is for one hour.

After that, each extra hour is charged at $100."

"Yes, I would like to come and look around. I've got some free time tomorrow, could I come around six? Would that be okay?"

"Yes that would be fine, madam. Can I ask your name?"

"Yes, it's Amy Hanson."

"Okay then Amy, I look forward to meeting you at six tomorrow. Have a lovely evening."

"Bye."

The minute I put the phone down I felt totally exhilarated. I couldn't believe I had really done it. I was going to have sex with a woman and the thought of it filled me with excitement. The fact that it was going to be with some pretty girl I'd never met made it even more of a turn on.

My pussy was hot and throbbing, and ached to be touched. I lay back on the bed, and pushing my hand up between my legs I felt the dampness of my panties with my fingertips. Pulling them to one side, I slid my fingers easily into my soaking wet pussy. I could see myself in the mirror on the wall opposite. My short summer cotton dress was up around my waist and my tanned bare legs pressed into the white sheet. I pulled my knees up to slip off my panties, and throwing them on the floor I saw the reflection of my glistening pussy in the mirror, I watched as my fingers thrust deeper and deeper inside. I kept thinking about the girl I'd choose, what she would look like and what she would do to me. As I was a brunette, I thought I'd choose a blonde. She'd have long fair hair, a beautiful face, firm breasts, and a cute little bum. And she would be so responsive to my touch, we would caress and cuddle, kissing each other softly from head to toe. I squeezed my thighs tightly together as I climaxed, massaging my clit between my fingers and pushing three fingers into my pussy.

Early the next morning, I got up and showered, I was nearly tempted to masturbate as I was so horny. I could think of nothing but The Angel Room.

I got through my morning appointments and then headed back into Manhattan to buy some especially sexy underwear. Once I was back in my hotel room, I tried on the lingerie and slipped a simple black dress over the top. I chose some high shiny black shoes. They look so sexy although they're not practical at all. I looked in the mirror. The dress showed off my figure, and outlined my breasts perfectly. I imagined the girl I would choose looking at me and licking her lips at the thought of fucking me. I lifted up my dress to see how the panties I'd bought fitted me. They were deliciously tight fitting, giving me a really sexy sensation. The black sheer nylon outlining my pussy lips. I quickly pulled the dress back down resisting the urge to rub my clitoris.

It was already twenty past five. It was a hot summers evening and the Angel Room was only a couple of blocks away, but I thought I would take a cab as I didn't want to arrive all hot and sweaty, although I hoped I would leave that way. I slung my bag on my shoulder and left.

The cab driver assumed I was a prostitute when I told him the area I wanted to go to.

"Just starting work then?"

"No, actually I'm visiting a friend."

I could tell by his glance in the mirror that he didn't believe me.

The cab pulled up near to The Angel Room. The road was full of big cars, most had well-muscled black guys sitting on the bonnets. The houses were turn of the century, three to four storeys high, with steps leading up to the front doors. The steps were littered with kids, running up and down. I paid the cab driver and opened the car door. My dress rode up as I stepped out and I pulled it back down into place as some guys whistled and jeered at me. I walked up the street looking for number 18. It was the last house on the street and set back from the others. As I approached the door I had butterflies in my stomach, but I was too excited to turn back.

The girl who let me in introduced herself as Emma. She was stunning, jet black hair, blue eyes and red lips. She had on the shortest dress, it barely covered her light blue panties which were always partially on show, depending on how she was standing.

"I rang yesterday about coming to have a look around," I said, sounding a bit nervous.

"Let's go for a tour around, and you can see what you think of us," said Emma taking my hand. She took me up

THE ANGEL ROOM

a stairway. Just as we reached the top a girl came out of one of the doors. She looked lovely. Shoulder length auburn hair in pigtails, with a really cute girly face. She was barely five foot tall but had very large breasts, she must have been a 38FF.

"Oh, hi Tammy," said Emma, "this is Amy, I'm just showing her around the place."

"Hi Amy. I love your dress, where d'ya get it?" Tammy asked running her fingers across the material.

"I bought it in England."

"I love your accent too, really sexy. I'd love to speak that way, it sounds so hot!"

Tammy went downstairs, and Emma took me into one of the bedrooms. Sitting on the bed, reading a book, was another beautiful girl. She couldn't have been more than twenty years old. Long blonde hair, big blue eyes, and a lovely smile. Her clothes were exquisite, very tight knee length black boots, the tiniest black panties and a stretch nylon light blue top with a zip up front.

"Amy, this is Jo," said Emma, "she's only been with us a couple of weeks. Jo works here on Fridays, the rest of the week she's an assistant editor at one of the big publishing houses."

"Hi Amy," said Jo putting her book down on the bed.

"Hi. It's nice to meet you. I have a friend in England who is a writer so I know quite a lot about the publishing business myself. My friend, Bettina, collects erotic stories."

"Really? I edit a lot of erotic stuff. I love it."

"What are you reading," I asked pointing to her book.

"It's 'Cherry's Secret Sex Garden' It must be good, it's made me really horny! I'd love you to stay Amy if you have some time."

I didn't need to see any of the other girls to make my choice. This was the girl of my fantasy.

"I'd love to," I replied, and Emma smiled at me and left us, closing the door behind her.

"I'll read you the bit that made me so horny Amy, where is it now, yes, here it is . . . *the two girls were at the height of their passion, their legs entwined, their pussies pressed together, their clits so sensitive as they pushed into each other* . . ."

As she read to me her hand beckoned me to sit next to her. I sat as close to her as I could, our thighs were touching. Jo was so sexy, every word she read sent shivers up and down my spine. She had the perfect hourglass figure, full rounded breasts, a small waist and firm soft thighs. She put the book down, turned towards me and gently kissed me on the lips.

"Come with me, I'll take you to the Angel Room. It's my favourite room, you'll love it too."

Jo took my hand and led me up a flight of stairs to the top of the house. She opened a blue door.

Inside, there must have been over a hundred candles lining the walls, creating the only light in the room. It was so beautiful.

"Wow! Jo this is lovely."

"I knew you'd like it," she said, closing the door behind us. In the centre of the room was a king size bed, covered with blue crushed velvet. Jo kissed me again on the lips, this time with passion and urgency. I opened my mouth and her tongue teased mine. She caressed my stomach with her hand, pulling my dress up to my waistline. She broke away and led me to the bed. Sitting next to me Jo unzipped the back of my dress, I stood up and let it fall to the floor.

"I love your lingerie Amy, here come and stand in front of me so I can touch you."

I did as she asked. She ran her hands over my panties, into the crack of my arse and softly pushed her fingertips into my pussy through the thin material.

"Ooh you're already nice and wet."

She slipped a finger inside my panties and ran it along my sex lips. Then she put the finger to her mouth and licked and sucked it.

"Umm, you taste really sweet, I'll have more of that a little later."

I pushed her back on to the bed and fell on top of her. I'd never felt such raw thoughts of sheer lust. I unzipped her top, her nipples were aroused, pert and pink.

"Lick them Amy, I love it, my nipples are so sensitive."

Again, I did as she asked. It was as if she was a real girlfriend, I really wanted to please her. I cupped her breast in my hand and flicked and teased her with my tongue, gently biting her hard nipple with my teeth. She writhed beneath me. I pushed my hand down the front of her panties, she was nice and wet.

"Oooh!" She cried as I slid two fingers into her cunt. It was so different to making love to a man, I knew exactly how to please her, I knew what she was feeling. I knew what she wanted.

"Let me taste your pussy again Amy." Jo turned me on to my back and eased my panties down. With both hands under my arse she lifted my pussy towards her mouth. Her tongue ran over my sex.

"Ooh you taste so sweet Amy," She pushed her tongue deeper. Her lips brushing my clitoris, sending electricity through my body. Now she concentrated on my clit, sucking and kissing. I was in heaven. I looked down and Jo was looking up at me, her mouth buried in my pussy. She pulled away.

"Mmm, that was nice," she said licking her lips. "You've got a gorgeous pussy, I could eat it all day."

"Please, eat me some more," I said. Turning on to my front I was on all fours with my arse in her face. I spread my legs wide so she had a good view of my dripping pussy.

"Eat me . . . Please . . ." I begged, feeling totally wanton, totally uninhibited.

I felt her hands on my inner thighs. Her hot breath on my sex. Then, her tongue pushed my lips apart and slid into my throbbing, burning cunt.

"Yes, yes, that's it. Tease me." I pushed myself hard into her face. Moving my arse up and down as Jo sucked and licked me. She had hold of my arse pulling the cheeks apart, her tongue sending wave upon wave of sheer desire and lust through my body. I could feel my orgasm, I quickly pulled myself away. I didn't want it to finish. I lay on my back.

"Jo, turn around so that I can taste you." I said trying to catch my breath, "We can taste each other."

She pulled off her panties and unzipped her boots. She looked so sexy.

"Wow, Amy I've never had so much fun," she said as she straddled me, her pussy just inches from my face. Jo leaned forward and immediately began to use her tongue on me. I gazed at her beautiful pussy, pink and glistening and so near to my mouth. I'd never gone down on another woman before, but it seemed so natural. Two women giving each other pleasure. I lifted my head and licked her sex lips. Jo sighed with pleasure, wriggling her arse from side to side. I rested my head back on the pillow and Jo slid herself back so her pussy was over my mouth. We were both in heaven greedily giving and receiving pleasure. I found her clit, sucking and licking it. Her moans got louder. I thought she was about to come when she lifted herself up off of me. She turned around and kissed me, our mouths wet with love juice. It was a beautiful moment. Then we were sitting facing each other, our legs entwined, our pussies touching, rubbing our clits together. Still kissing, our orgasms were building. Jo leaned forward and from under a pillow she produced a double headed dildo. It looked like a crystal but smooth with two bulbous ends, it was about twelve inches from tip to tip.

"Let's use this," she said.

I nodded in agreement. We edged apart slightly. She gently pushed one end slowly into her pussy.

"Oooh, yeah that feels good."

Half the dildo had gone into her cunt. I took hold of the other end and eased my pussy on to it. Again our pussies were touching.

"Feels good doesn't it Amy."

"Yes . . . it . . . sure . . . does!" I gasped trying to focus.

"Let's look into each others eyes while we come Amy, I love that."

"I think I'm . . . yes Jo . . . I'm coming, now, now!"

"Yes, yes Amy, now now. Oooh yes."

We both began to grind and thrust our cunts into one another. We kissed, our eyes transfixed. Jo's beautiful face was glowing in ecstacy. We both climaxed simultaneously, caressing and loving every lust-filled second. It seemed to go on forever. Finally exhausted, we both fell backwards on to the bed.

"Wow, I can't believe I just did that." I giggled.

Jo sat up, "that was the best, that's why I come here, to fuck with gorgeous women like you Amy. That was great wasn't it?"

"It certainly was. It felt fantastic, I've never, well you're my first woman."

We fell into each others arms laughing.

Bettina writes,

The last time I went into my Building Society I could tell that the Manager had something else on his mind other than his work. I know him rather well and he is always most charming to me. He knows what I do for a living and he just looked like someone with a big secret. It took me some delicate coaxing and a lunch date for him to open up to me. But once he began, he told me everything . . .

Red Obsession

RED OBSESSION

"She's there again Taylor," said Jane as she passed the open office door.

Taylor stood up and walked to the large glass window that overlooked the counters. Yes, she was there, standing by the door with her back against the wall, just looking across at him.

"What are you going to do?" asked Emma, glancing up from her computer screen. "She can't stand there all day."

"She's not doing any harm Emma."

"But it's not exactly normal behaviour is it? Most people come here to actually pay money in or draw it out. I'm sure she's one sandwich short of a picnic."

Taylor walked along the glass window to collect some files from the table and the girl's eyes followed him. He walked back and saw her follow him again.

"She's staring at you . . ." Emma said, pressing him for some action.

"I know, I know."

"Why don't you call security?"

"I already sent someone out to her a few days ago. She just said she was waiting for someone."

"Well you've got to do something, it's too weird."

"She's not exactly doing anything wrong .." said Taylor as he sat down and tried to attend to his papers. His eyes scanned the pages but his thoughts rested firmly with the girl. He could see her clearly in his mind. Her face was beautiful and unusual. Although her dress was knee length and plain, it fitted tightly to her body and showed a curvy figure. Taylor had thought about her a lot in the past days that she'd been hanging around the building.

Taylor caught sight of his refection in the glass. His newly grown beard and moustache gave him a distinguished air he had decided. But the lights reflected a glare on his balding head bringing him back to the ground with a jolt. To have receded so much by the age of thirty-five was, he thought, a cruel trial. But it was a curse on his whole family. He was sure she couldn't be interested in him, but the way she gazed at him allowed him to at least fantasize otherwise.

"Coffee?"

"No, thanks Emma."

"I'm just going to make some for the girls," she said, disappearing out the door.

Taylor got up, secretly hoping as he glanced across the branch office floor that the girl was still exactly where she had been. She was. She stared into his face, her lips parted slightly. Taylor pressed the security intercom, and immediately was answered.

"Problem?"

"No, not really . . . the girl by the door, you know the one, could you go and ask her to step into my office?"

"Will do."

"Oh, and Ben, don't frighten her, be nice."

Taylor saw Ben come out of the security office and go over to the girl. She listened to him and then obediently followed him to the back office without a word.

Taylor watched her approach and felt strangely nervous. He'd built up quite a personality for her in his head. She stood quietly, and seemed to be inspecting his every move with great interest.

"I wonder if there is anything we can help you with Miss? Are you waiting for something or someone?"

"I was."

"You mean, you're not anymore?"

"No."

As she spoke, she reached out and took Taylor's right hand. She held it lightly, stroking his fingers and studying them carefully. It wasn't a usual kind of encounter and Taylor couldn't quite get his bearings. Was it his imagination that she seemed so sexually aroused; her cheeks were flushed and her lips reddening.

"Miss . ."

"My name is Sky"

"Sky? That's a lovely name." It seemed lame, but Taylor didn't know what else to say.

"Perhaps you are wanting to open an account?"

"Of sorts."

"Well I can help you with that."

"That's what I'm counting on." Sky looked into Taylor's eyes. She pressed his fingers to her lips and licked across his fingertips. Undoing the top three buttons on her dress, she opened it enough to guide Taylor's hand inside. He felt the warm softness of her breast and the hard point of her nipple as his fingers brushed over it. As his hand touched her skin, her eyes closed and her mouth opened to draw a sharp breath.

"I need to see you later," she said, "when you leave here."

"I leave at six."

"I know. I'll be outside."

Sky buttoned her blouse, turned and walked slowly out of the building society. Taylor's fly was stretched over his stiffened cock which begged for some urgent attention. He went across the shop floor to the toilet. He unzipped his fly. Taking his shaft in his hand, he brought himself off, as he imagined fucking Sky. Pushing his penis hard into her pussy. He imagined her wanting all he could give her, until she could take no more.

Taylor found the afternoon very long. He couldn't concentrate. All he could think about was Sky, and how she'd acted in the office. Emma asked him how he got rid of 'that girl' and he didn't exactly know what to say. He told her that Sky had mistaken him for someone else, someone she knew. It didn't seem so far-fetched to him either, considering that girls don't usually throw themselves at him.

At six o'clock Taylor was ready to leave. He kept

looking outside but couldn't see Sky. Perhaps she wasn't going to be there after all. As he left the building society, he saw her standing in a nearby doorway. She had a bright red dress on, red shoes and red lipstick. She looked stunning.

"Come with me," said Sky, taking his hand and leading him to a black cab waiting at the kerb. She spoke quietly to the driver and then got into the back seat. Taylor followed and sat beside her. He felt a little uneasy.

"Relax," said Sky smiling, "be content. I only want to make you happy, that's all."

Sky stroked Taylor's face and then kissed him gently. His pulse quickened and he wanted to take hold of her but he held back. As her gentle kisses caressed his lips, her fingers slid down to his belt and began to undo it. Her forwardness surprised but excited him. His erection pressed upwards against his fly, and was desperate to reach her hand as her fingers eased down the zip and slipped inside. As they touched the length and hardness of his erection, Sky whispered something in a foreign language. Taylor didn't know what it was but it sounded sexy to him. Sky took his cock in her hands, gripping it gently as she lowered her head down towards it. Taylor felt her lips find the tip of his cock, it stiffened even more and stretched to get inside her mouth. She didn't let it in at first. Her red lips just took in the very tip of his erection and her tongue began to circle gently. Her lipstick came off on to his shaft and she licked it off. Then she let his cock slide between her lips, and travel right to the back of her throat. Taylor felt the warmth and wetness of her mouth encapsulate his erection. He watched her lips, bright red, stretched around its girth, as she sucked on him hard, with long, smooth movements. Her breathing was fast, and she was so turned on in pleasing him and taking him into her mouth that Taylor knew that he couldn't take much more. The sight of his cock disappearing inside her mouth and reappearing again was bringing him to burning point. His cock swelled and he ejaculated deep inside her mouth, sending his white creamy cum into her throat. Sky took it all and swallowed it down. Smiling, she sat up.

Taylor realised he'd forgotten about the cab driver, and now began to wonder if he'd watched them in the mirror. He looked around to see where the cab had taken them, it was his own road, and the cab driver was pulling up to the kerb just beside Taylor's house.

Taylor opened the door and stepped out of the cab.

"I'll see you tomorrow," said Sky as she took a card out of her pocket and handed it to Taylor. "Here is my address. Come to my flat tomorrow night. You will come won't you?"

"Yes, but . ."

"I just want to make you happy," Sky reassured. She smiled, and the cab pulled away.

"Sky . ."

Taylor was glad that she didn't answer him as he didn't know what he was going to say anyway. He went into his house and threw himself on the sofa. What on earth was going on? Could she really want *him* that badly? It would seem so. And oh *how* she wanted him! She couldn't help herself. He really must have charmed her, big time. He replayed the day's events in his mind, and thought of her in that red dress in the cab, with his cock in her mouth. Nothing like it had ever happened to him before. He had never come in a woman's mouth before, all his previous girlfriends had refused to do it. 'I just want to make you happy' she had said. As he pondered the words, Taylor felt a chill begin to creep up his spine. That's probably exactly what prostitutes say, he thought. Now it made far more sense. She was a prostitute, and after she'd lured him to her flat, she'd ask for lots of money for her services, or worse still her pimp would rob him. But why the visits to the building society? Surely there were easier targets. She wanted *him*. He looked at the card she gave him. It was scrappy, and the address was in handwriting. This reassured him somewhat, at least it wasn't a printed card. He allowed his ego to regain control of his mind; it's not every day a strange and beautiful girl wants you desperately. He replayed the blow job in his imagination as his hand closed around his erection.

The day passed so slowly as Taylor clock-watched; when would it ever be six? Taylor couldn't focus on his work. It all seemed unimportant anyway, and just a distraction from Sky. She was all he wanted to think about. He often looked at the door to see if she was there, watching him, but she didn't come.

At six he went home. He showered and changed. As he drove to Sky's address he wondered what the evening would be like. What if the door was answered by her slimy pimp? Taylor decided it was time to lay his fears aside and get back to allowing himself to believe he really was the object of her desire. It was much more enjoyable!

He arrived at her flat in Finchley Road. Sky opened the door.

"Come in," she said, smiling and taking his hand to lead him into a large room. It was tidy and spacious, with a high ceiling. There were two other doorways and through one he could see a small kitchen. Sky made a drink and came and sat by him on a large comfortable sofa.

"I'm so glad you came," she said, "drink this and relax."

Taylor took the glass. He looked round the room. One wall was a mass of bookshelves from the floor to the ceiling. Taylor noticed a plaque above one of the doorways, it read, 'Without books there is no knowledge'.

"You like books," Taylor said, stating the obvious.

"Yes I love them. Words are everything. Knowledge is everything. You must write, you have the hands for it."

"No, I couldn't. I wouldn't know what to write about."

"Write the truth as you see it," said Sky taking his hand and stroking it. "These hands shouldn't be wasted. There is so much you have to say. You won't know until you try."

Sky began to stroke Taylor's thighs and her hands lingered close to his fly.

"Lie back, relax, let me please you."

Taylor did as she asked. Sky was beautiful. He watched her take off her dress; revealing a red bra, red panties, red suspender belt and black stockings. She threw her dress aside and sat astride his lap. Above the stocking tops, the white flesh of her thighs pressed against his suit, and he ran his hands upwards over her legs to her hips. Sky began to undo Taylor's tie. He looked at her breasts squeezed into the lacy bra, they were rounded and creamy white. He brought his hands up to feel their softness, and Sky whispered something he didn't understand. She pulled his tie from around his neck and let it fall between her legs, moving her hand round to pull it tightly upwards behind her. It pressed into her panties, up into the crack of her arse and into the folds of her pussy, and she gently pulled it back and forth Taylor watched her masturbate with his tie. Her mouth was red and shiny and he wanted her badly. He began to unbutton his shirt, but Sky put her hand over his.

"Leave it on, leave your suit on . . . please."

Her fingers trailed down to his fly and released his erection. It sprang up to meet her open lips as she bent over him and took him in her mouth. She sucked him gently for a minute or two, then unclipped her bra, let his wet penis slide out of her mouth and down between her breasts. She pressed her breasts together tightly around his cock and firmly massaged it up and down. Then she laid back on the sofa and guided Taylor to lean over her and place his cock back between her breasts. This way she could touch the end of it with her tongue each time it pushed upwards. Taylor whispered to her that she was beautiful and her work on him became more intense. Taylor felt the rise of his semen, and looked down to see it shoot from his cock towards Sky's open mouth. She put out her tongue and he watched his hot cum fill her mouth as it pumped out of him.

Sky sat up. Cum oozing from her lovely full lips.

"You will come back tomorrow evening won't you?" she said. Taylor hadn't had time to catch his breath.

"Yes, I'll be here," he said.

Taylor sat at his desk. Work held no interest for him. He thought only of Sky and their time together the previous evening. He thought about what she had said about writing. Perhaps he did have something to say, but he just hadn't realised it yet. He picked up a pen and turned over his pile of photocopied figure-work. He began to write - just anything that came into his head. He felt like he was in a dream state, a waking dream, and he wrote page after page, without even knowing what he was writing about. The words flowed but he couldn't sense them or read them. He put the pages in his briefcase and then it was six o'clock.

Arriving at Sky's flat, he rang the bell and waited. He noticed the name plate under the bell, it read 'Krupskaya'.

Sky opened the door and invited him in, as she had the night before. Taylor sat on the sofa and took a drink again.

"Is that your full name, Krupskaya?

"Yes. I shorten it to Sky, it's easier."

Relaxed on the sofa, Taylor felt at home. He began to feel like he never wanted to go back to his own flat. He took the papers out of his briefcase and laid them on the coffee table, as it he was in his own place. As he drank, Sky picked up his papers and began to read them.

"These are wonderful! You are so clever. Now you are properly using your talents." Sky took Taylor's hand in hers, "Come into the bedroom," she said, removing what little clothing she was wearing as she walked.

Taylor followed her through the doorway. She put his papers down on the dressing table. Taylor looked around. The room was full of small statues, bronze busts, velvet red banners and flags.

Sky turned on a tape of music, with a man delivering a Russian speech. She lay on the bed and held her hand out towards Taylor.

"Come to me Vladimir, make love to me."

Vladimir? Taylor glanced down at his papers and saw some of the words jumping out at him,

'proletariat' . . 'bourgeoisie' . . . 'the exploitation of one class by another'. . .

He looked into the mirror, and saw what she saw when she looked at him - Lenin.

Taylor went to her. She was hot, and desperate for his

touch. He touched her, and she cried out Russian words. He kissed her deeply and caressed her breasts. He took control, leaning back and undoing his trousers. Her passion for him turned him on so much. Pushing her thighs apart just enough to guide his cock towards her pussy, he slid it inside her pussy lips. It was so tight and felt so good. She pressed her thighs together, creating an even tighter friction. This was to arousing for Taylor; he didn't want to come too quickly. He withdrew. "Kneel on the bed," he whispered and Sky turned around to kneel on all fours. He caressed her bottom. It was luxuriously soft and pale. She was speaking to him in Russian in a breathy voice. She turned to look at him behind her.

"Fuck me . . . I can't wait . . . fuck me now . . . I want you to be the first to have me . . . please now." Sky was so hot and so turned on. Taylor leaned forward and kissed her back and then trailed small kisses down over the creamy white cheeks of her bottom, driving her to the edge with his teasing. He held apart her swollen pussy lips with his fingertips and slipped his tongue inside. Sky cried out. He teased her and withdrew his tongue, to slip it softly inside again.

"Harder . . . deeper!" she cried.

Taylor withdrew his tongue and instead gave her his cock, stiff and hard, it penetrated her deeply as he pressed down on her buttocks with his large sensitive hands. His thrusts were fast and hard, and he had Sky screaming as he thrust into her, his spunk welling up as she cried out in her ecstasy. He shot his cum deep inside her and as he finally withdrew, it dripped from her red pussy lips, down her white thighs. She massaged it into her skin then licked her fingers.

Taylor opened his eyes. The sun was blazing through the blinds. He looked at Sky sleeping by his side, and he stroked her hair. She stirred gently and opened her eyes, to smile as soon as she saw his face.

"Come Krupskaya," said Taylor, "there is much to do."

Candy writes,

Don't you find that sometimes you meet the most interesting and lovely people completely by chance? Bettina invited me to London and showed me the places she likes to shop. We were in Skin Two, when we overheard a conversation between two beautiful girls. It sounded like they'd been up to something really naughty. Not wanting to ever miss out on something naughty, Bettina went to talk to them. Their names were Lucy and Sara, and they had quite a tale to tell . . .

Just Press Play

JUST PRESS PLAY

The man was behind Lucy now, thrusting his cock into her cunt. She could see his contorted face reflected in the mirror in front of her, at least one of them was enjoying it. Lucy reached round to tickle his balls as he slapped into her. She gasped and cried, "Yes, yes, fuck me, yes harder, you're so big, oh yes I'm going to, ooh!" She thought this would make him come a bit quicker.

"Oh yes, you fucking whore!" he shouted, "you fucking bitch."

Lucy felt his cock spasm inside her pussy and within twenty seconds it was all over. He pulled his limp prick out of her, and she handed him a tissue. She watched as he slowly pulled the condom off and wiped his tiny cock.

"Put that in the bin, and when you're dressed the maid will show you out. I had a lovely time, make sure you come again. I'll be looking forward to it." She turned and opened the door leaving it slightly ajar as she left. In a loud voice that she knew he would hear, she said, "Sara, that was the best fuck I've ever had, I'm worn out."

"Well, you'd better sit down and have a rest. After I've shown the gentleman out I'll make you a cup of coffee. Here, rub some of this soothing cream into your pussy, it will calm it down." Sara grinned. Both girls desperately tried not to laugh, as Sara showed the man out, telling him what a great lover he must be to have worn Lucy out.

"What a wanker he was! And you should have seen the size of his prick, it was the size of a MacDonald's French fry. I thought the rubber was just going to fall off." Lucy picked up the thirty pounds and put it in a tin on the bookcase.

"Here's your coffee, don't let it get cold," said Sara. "Your next client's at two o'clock, oh and I bought some of those biscuits you're always going on about. You know the ones with the cream in the middle. I'll go and get them."

Lucy reclined on the sofa. She was still wearing just her black lace panties and hold-up stockings. "Who's coming at two?" she asked.

"Oh it's that tall ugly bloke, Mr Jones, although I think he'll be arriving at two and coming a short while later!" Both girls laughed.

"I bet that's not his real name. You'd think he could think up something better than Jones," said Lucy.

"Yeah, like Ugly Bastard," snapped Sara.

"I think I'll relax for an hour before he gets here." Lucy closed her eyes, spread herself on the sofa, and drifted off to sleep.

"Wake up Lucy, Mr Jones just pressed the intercom. He's just got in the elevator".

"Alright, bring him in here while I get ready in the

bedroom. Give me a few minutes."

Lucy tidied the bedclothes and put on some more lipstick. When she was ready she opened the bedroom door.

"Ah Mr Jones, it's so good to see you. I've been laying here frustrated all morning just waiting for you. My pussy is aching." Lucy pushed her hand down the front of her knickers. "I really need a good fuck."

Mr Jones stepped through the doorway past Lucy and into the bedroom. Sara held up the cash she'd got from him and both girls smiled.

"Ooh Mr Jones I'm feeling horny as hell. I hope you've got a nice stiff cock to fuck me with. Here, let me help you with those clothes and we can get started."

"I'd prefer to keep my shirt on if that's alright with you."

"Just as long as you let me get to your gorgeous cock," said Lucy.

Mr Jones undid his belt and placed it neatly on a chair. Then he pulled down his trousers, carefully folded them and put them on the chair. Lucy tried to hide her amusement. Finally he took off his Y-fronts, folded them and placed them on top of his trousers.

"Do you want your usual? Mr Jones. Me on top talking dirty, impaled on your hard cock."

"Yes that would be fine," he replied.

Mr Jones lay on the bed. Lucy seductively pulled down her panties and stepped out of them. She climbed on to the bed straddling his legs just below his penis.

"Ooh Mr Jones, let's get your cock nice and hard."

BETTINA AND CANDY

Lucy took it in her hand and rubbed up and down its shaft. She could feel it getting harder, soon it was fully erect.

"That's better Mr Jones, your cock's nice and stiff." Lucy leaned forward with the condom between her teeth and covered his erect penis with the thin rubber. She had done it so many times that she was an expert. "Now I'm going to squat over it and slide it into my hot wet pussy. Watch it Mr Jones, watch it push past my sex lips. Ooh yes, see how it's sliding in. It's so hard, and so big. My pussy is so hot, can you feel it Mr Jones?"

"Yes I can Lucy, keep talking," he replied.

"Pinch my nipples Mr Jones. Take them between your fingers, hurt me, give me pain and pleasure. Yes that's it, it's lovely." Lucy sucked on her fingers, giving Mr Jones exactly what he had paid for. That's why he was one of her regulars.

"I love to fuck like this Mr Jones, to feel your hard cock sliding into my cunt. You're so hard, so virile. Can you feel my pussy tightening around your cock? Oh yes, I really needed this, straddling your hard prick. I've never been fucked like this before. You're magnificent Mr Jones!"

Lucy was now playing with her clitoris, pushing her fingers into it in a circular motion. She knew that this usually would take Mr Jones over the edge. Lucy could see he was about to come. He never made any noise, just a slight quickening in his breathing, and it was over.

"Well Mr Jones, thank you very much for that. As you could see I was gagging for a good fuck. Thank God

JUST PRESS PLAY

you rang and made the appointment."

Lucy got some tissues from the dresser and handed them to Mr Jones. "You always get me so worked up Mr Jones. I don't know how I would manage if you stopped coming. Get dressed and Sara will show you out. I'll look forward to your next appointment, don't leave it too long now will you?"

"Me and Mrs Jones are going away for a couple of weeks, but I promise to ring as soon as I get back."

Lucy left the bedroom and flopped on to the sofa. Sara showed Mr Jones to the door. "Goodbye Mr Jones. Have a nice holiday," she said and closed the door.

"Are there any of those biscuits left or have you scoffed the lot while I was busy?" asked Lucy.

"No there's still more than half the packet left. Anyway, I can afford to put on some weight." Sara picked up the packet and playfully tossed them at Lucy.

"Ah, my favourites," sighed Lucy.

"I've been thinking of a way that we can get more money out of the punters," said Sara.

"What, you're finally going to do a double act with me? We would get twice as much money if we fucked each other, and then both of us were fucked by the punter."

"No not that, stop going on about it. I hear it morning, noon and night."

"Well it's a damned good idea, we'd make a fortune. We are both absolutely gorgeous. Most of the men who come here want to fuck you. If they knew you had never been fucked by a man they'd pay twice as much."

"You know I want my first time with a man to be special. I'm only eighteen, I've got plenty of time."

"Come over here, and tell me your idea. Make us both rich."

Sara sat on the floor and rested her head in Lucy's lap.

"Well, while you were fucking Mr Jones, I checked out our site on the internet to see if we could spice it up a bit. I started looking around other Escort's sites and I came across this American girl's site. I think her name was Cindy. Here I'll show you, I've bookmarked her page."

They went over to the computer, and Sara soon had Cindy's site on the screen.

"This is the part that interested me. Look Lucy, she does a service where the punter can take home a video of himself having sex with her, and look how much she charges. We could do the same thing, all we would need is a video camera, a couple of lights and some blank video tapes. I could do the filming, I could dress up in some sexy outfit so I wouldn't look out of place. I'm sure we'd have punters queuing up."

"We could charge a hundred pounds for a half hour tape!" exclaimed Lucy. "How soon could we start?"

"As soon as I've bought the equipment and posted the new service on the web. I'll buy the stuff this afternoon."

"I'll come with you."

"No, you can't, you've got Mark coming at three."

Sara picked up all the cash they had and left. Lucy made everything tidy in the bedroom, then switched on the television and watched some boring programme for housewives.

Lucy heard the buzzer and pressed the intercom. It was Mark.

"Come up, I've been waiting for you," Lucy said seductively. She greeted him wearing just her black panties and stockings. To her surprise he had someone with him.

"I hope you don't mind Lucy but I've got a mate with me. I told him what a great fuck you were and he wanted to come along. We thought you could do us both at the same time, or if you don't do that you can have us one at a time."

"Well I charge a bit extra, it will be eighty pounds for you both together or thirty pounds each separately."

"Here's eighty." Both men pulled some notes from their pockets and handed them to Lucy.

"Go into the bedroom boys and take your clothes of. I'll be with you in a minute." Lucy lit a cigarette and had a quick drag before stubbing it out in an ashtray. She checked herself out in the mirror, long thick auburn hair, big brown eyes, large firm boobs and a tiny waist. What more could any man want she thought smiling at her reflection. She pulled up her panties, so they went into the crack of her bum and straightened the stocking tops. "There, that's it," she said to herself.

Lucy could hear laughing coming from the bedroom. She pushed the door open and there stood Mark and Jake stark naked in front of her.

"You have got half an hour, so how do you want to

start?" asked Lucy.

"I thought I'd watch while you give Jake a blowjob and then we can just take it from there," said Mark.

"Okay Jake, lay on the bed." Lucy went to the table, took a rubber and placed it in her mouth. She climbed on to the bed between Jake's legs, took his cock in her hand. Leaning forward she slowly took his penis into her mouth covering it with the rubber. Lucy massaged the base of his shaft with her hands whilst sliding her lips up and down its length. Jake had his eyes closed and a smile creased his face. Mark was standing to one side watching Lucy's mouth slide up and down, he had his cock in his hand slowly pulling the foreskin backwards and forwards. Lucy looked up towards Jake and he opened his eyes. She thought he was quite good looking, with a muscular body, the type of bloke she would go for if she was in a club. In his mid-twenties and clean. She could feel herself becoming sexually aroused, she felt a dampness between her legs, something that she rarely felt with punters. She sucked and teased with more intensity, everything became a blur all she could think about was Jake's cock, to give him pleasure was her only thought.

Suddenly Lucy was aware of two hands pulling her knickers down, pushing her legs apart and lifting her arse up. Then she felt Mark's penis push its way into her cunt. She pushed back on to it, taking its full length. Mark's hands held on to her hips as he thrust into her. Lucy's pussy was on fire, suddenly it dawned on her that Mark wasn't wearing a condom.

"What the fuck are you playing at Mark? You know I don't have sex without a condom," Lucy shouted.

"I forgot Lucy, look I'll put one on, see."

"I've a good mind to chuck you both out. If you weren't regulars and I wasn't so turned on, I would. Now fuck me some more and finish me off."

Mark and Jake changed positions. Mark was kneeling, with his cock in Lucy's mouth, and Jake was behind her ramming his cock into her pussy. Lucy found her clitoris, "Oh fuck me Jake . . . fuck me, hard!" she cried.

She was wanking Mark off with her hand now, she pulled the condom off. "Shoot your spunk in my face Mark," before she had finished saying the words semen spurted from Mark's cock splattering her face with cum. Mark fell back on to the bed exhausted. Lucy frantically rubbed her clit, she could feel her own orgasm starting to rush through her body. Jake pulled her hips towards him grinding his cock into her pussy as he ejaculated.

"What a fuck!" he announced.

Lucy was now kneeling between them, one hand fucking herself the other rubbing her clit. "Oh yes, yes! I'm coming . . . yes, yes . . . now!" Lucy arched her back and screamed wildly, she felt her own juices as they trickled from her pussy.

"Wow, that was a good one, one of the best," Lucy gasped. "You boys sure know how to show a girl a good time. I don't think I'll be able to work for a few days, my pussy's so sore." She went over to the sink and washed the semen off her face. Mark and Jake got dressed.

BETTINA AND CANDY

"Well I hope I'll see you both again, though perhaps one at a time, I don't think I've got the strength to do that again! Then again, it was good wasn't it?"

Just as Lucy was letting the boys out, Sara came in.

"Did Mark bring someone with him? Are you okay? Did you have to do them both?"

"Yes, and I'm fine, and I quite enjoyed it. Did you see Jake leaving? He was quite a dish wasn't he? I even had an orgasm! I think that's only the second one I've had while I've been working. It felt dangerous. You not being here as well added to the risk, it was more exciting. But I won't be doing that again!"

"I bought everything we need, and it's all going to be delivered last thing today, about six," declared Sara. "There's no more punters today, so we can set everything up and see if it works."

"I'll put some clothes on, and change these knickers." Lucy slipped them off and threw them at Sara. "Stick them in the washing machine will you, I'm going to take a shower."

Sara caught the panties, and looked at the gusset. "Ooh look they're soaked through with your cum." She lifted the panties to her face. "You smell delicious! Before you take a shower let me taste your pussy."

Lucy walked towards Sara and stood in front of her. Sara knelt down and slid both hands between Lucy's inner thighs and gently pushed her legs apart revealing the pinkness of her pussy lips. They were still wet and swollen from the sex. Sara's tongue tasted the sweetness of Lucy's cunt. Lucy pushed herself further into Sara's face, and Sara's tongue penetrated deeper. "You always taste better after you've come," Sara cooed, taking a deep breath.

"I really must take a shower, I feel so dirty and sweaty. We can get back to this later when we're trying out the video camera." Lucy rushed to the shower leaving Sara licking her lips.

Lucy had just stepped out of the shower when the intercom buzzed.

"Who is it?" Lucy asked.

"The delivery man with your video equipment Miss. Can I bring it up?"

"Yes, push the door."

Lucy and Sara were both waiting at the door when the man staggered in carrying three large boxes. Sara was fully dressed but Lucy was standing there dripping wet, with a tiny towel wrapped around her, just managing to cover her tits and arse.

"Where do you want these then girls?"

"Take them in the bedroom," said Lucy pointing the way.

"Do you want me to unpack them and give you a quick demonstration? It wouldn't take long. Besides, this is my last delivery of the day."

"Yeah, that would be great, eh Sara," Lucy said. "Then we can start using it straight away."

Lucy sat on the bed while Sara helped the delivery man undo the boxes.

"Shall I set the lights up to illuminate the bed?"

"Yeah that's where most of the action takes place!" said Sara, laughing. "You'd better watch him Lucy, he'll have you staring in a porn film."

"I'd be the hottest star to hit the silver screen," pouted Lucy, letting the top of the towel fall to show a hint of nipple. "What do you think Mr Director, will I do?"

"You sure are the sexiest thing I've seen in a long while," he stammered, blushing. "Just let me put a tape in the camera and I'll show you how it works. There that's it." He held the camera up and looked through the view finder, pointing it at Lucy. Lucy couldn't help herself, she was a born exhibitionist. She let the towel drop away and caressed her breasts, rubbing her now erect nipples between her fingers. She sucked on a finger and pouted for the camera.

"Does it record sound as well?" asked Sara.

"Oh yes, here is the microphone. I'll switch it on." He pointed to a section at the front of the camera, but didn't stop filming Lucy, who was now on all fours, her head nearest the camera with one hand between her legs, masturbating. "Ooh yes, that's lovely. I think I'm coming, yes, yes... ooh!" cried Lucy, now playing to the microphone as well as the lens.

"Have you finished mucking about Lucy? We've still got the website to update, and I'm sure this man has got other things to do," scolded Sara.

"Oh no, don't worry about me, I'm really enjoying myself, and as I said, you're my last delivery."

"And I bet you'd like to deliver more than the video equipment," said Lucy looking at the bulge in the delivery man's trousers. "Well perhaps, another time," she added.

Lucy got off the bed and handed him a card. It read: LUSCIOUS LUCY, YOUNG BUSTY BRUNETTE, 20 YEARS OLD, UNHURRIED SERVICE, FRIENDLY, KINKY AND VERY HORNY, I'M WAITING FOR YOUR CALL 768 410.

"Give me a ring sometime, we can have some fun. You could video me while I'm sucking your cock."

"I didn't know you were a . . . er . . ." he stuttered.

Lucy finished his sentence. "A good time girl? Oh yes, I would give you a really good time!"

He tucked the card safely into his pocket, and let himself out.

"Wow! That was fun, did you see the look on his face? I thought he was going to come in his pants," said Lucy, smiling wickedly.

"My panties are soaking wet. Watching you on the bed really turned me on. I'll put the video camera on the tripod and we'll film ourselves having sex."

Sara checked the camera was filming the bed, switched it on, and started to take her clothes off. She had a nice firm shapely body. Her tits were pert, with large pink nipples that always seemed to be pointing upwards. She had a well rounded bum and a lovely tight pussy. With shoulder length blonde hair and blue eyes, she could have any man she wanted, but by choice she was still a virgin. She had only ever been intimate with Lucy. They had met at college, both studying art history, but they found it too boring so they quit just before their final year. Now they shared a flat, Sara did all the publicity and running around and Lucy sold sex. Much more exciting.

"If we're on video we had better put on a bit of a show, we don't want to be disappointed when we see it," said Lucy. "Is the sound on?"

Sara, now naked, checked the button was pushed in. Lucy stared straight into the lens and announced, "Sara and Lucy fucking each other, take one."

Sara pushed Lucy back, so they were in the missionary position. She started to grind her pussy into Lucy's, slowly and rhythmically, so that their clits rubbed together. They kissed, open mouthed, biting and teasing each others lips. They rolled over, now Lucy was on top, she kissed and sucked Sara's nipples. She ran her hand down Sara's tummy, through her pubic hair to her sex lips and ran a finger along them, parting them gently, feeling the wetness inside.

"Fuck me Lucy, fuck me now . . . please!"

Lucy pushed two, then three fingers into Sara's pussy, slowly pushing them in and out.

"Yes, that's it."

Suddenly the phone started to ring in the other room. The answer machine kicked in, "Hello, this is Lucy and Sara's place. We can't come to the phone right now, we're busy. Please leave a message and we'll get back to you as soon as possible. Thanks."

"Yeah we're busy having a good fuck," gasped Sara. "Let's go down on each other for the camera."

Lucy twisted around so that her head was positioned just over Sara's pussy, and her pussy was just over Sara's mouth.

"You smell good," cooed Sara. She parted Lucy's buttocks and licked around her cunt pushing her tongue into her sweetness, tasting as much as she could. Lucy was teasing Sara's clitoris, flicking and licking it.

"Oh God Lucy! Stop or I'm going to come," cried Sara. "Oh it's too late! Lucy, lick me, suck me, I can't stop it. I'm coming! Yes yes, ooh yes." Sara's orgasm ripped through her, leaving her lying exhausted on the bed. "That was amazing Lucy, the best."

Lucy opened the bedside table drawer and took out her favourite vibrator, eight inches of smooth silver. She switched it on and turned towards the camera. Squatting down with her legs apart she ran the head over her clitoris, and along her pussy lips. She suddenly felt Sara's hand slide under her bottom. From behind, Sara was lightly caressing her arse circling her tight hole with her fingers. Lucy turned her head, "You naughty girl Sara, you know how much that excites me, keep going, yes that's it, don't stop, ooh yes."

Sara lay down so Lucy was now squatting over her face. She could use her tongue as well as her fingers. Lucy had pushed the vibrator inside her pussy, gently massaging the lips apart, letting her excitement build.

"Oh Sara, I can't hold back any longer, I've got to come. . . yes now!"

Sara licked harder, teasing Lucy's arse with her slender fingers. Lucy pushed the vibrator further into her cunt. She came powerfully, shuddering to her climax.

"Aahh, yes, now I'm totally shagged out! My pussy is burning from so much pleasure. I can't wait to see the video. I'll make some dinner," said Lucy, "then we'll curl up on the sofa and watch ourselves."

"As long as you don't make those horrible lentil fritters. You know how much I hate them. Make a pizza, I think we've got all the ingredients, and there's a ready-made base in the refrigerator."

"Alright," said Lucy, getting a clean pair of knickers out of the drawer. "What do you think of these Sara? Sexy or what? I bought them yesterday from that new shop that has just opened. The sales girl in there is gorgeous, short bobbed hair, full lips, and she wears glasses, they make her look *so* sexy. You know how I'm a sucker for girls who wear glasses. I'm going to go in there every day and buy one item of lingerie. I'll see if I can chat her up. I could bring her home, we could have a threesome."

"If she's as cute as you say she is, I'll come with you to the shop and have a look," said Sara.

After dinner, Sara pushed the tape into the video recorder.

"Wow, look at you Sara, you horny bitch, you're so fucking sexy, don't you think so?" cried Lucy, sitting forward on the sofa to get a better look.

"Yeah, I do look good, I must be photogenic or something."

"Look at your bum Sara, it's beautiful. We'll have to do a double act . . ."

"Not that again Lucy, I've told you I want my first fuck with a man to be special. I'll do the videoing but that's all."

The phone started to ring.

"Let the answerphone get it, I'm too tired for any more punters. When we've watched the video shall we have an early night? To sleep I mean, no sex."

"Yeah, okay, you look a bit tired. Oh look Lucy, you've got the vibrator. The punters are gonna love this. You go to bed and I'll set up the web page.

Sara was having breakfast when the telephone rang.

"Hello, how may I help you?" said Sara.

"Is that the massage service?"

"Yes, would you like some details?"

"Yes."

"The model's name is Lucy. She is a stunning brunette, very pretty. Her measurements are 36c 24 34. Lucy is 20 years old, 5 feet 8 inches in height. She has a bubbly personality, is very gentle and caring and takes her time."

"She sounds lovely."

"Lucy offers a range of services, although she doesn't do anal. Her fees start at forty pounds for half an hour, or

BETTINA AND CANDY

there is a VIP service which lasts for one hour, this is seventy-five pounds. You can also have your time here videoed for an extra fifty pounds. Would you like me to arrange a time for you to come and see her?"

"Yes, could I come at eleven thirty? A half hour will be fine. Could you tell me, would Lucy let me touch her intimately?"

"Oh yes. I know some girls don't like it, but Lucy loves a reverse massage. Eleven thirty will be fine, we'll see you then. Goodbye." Sara put down the phone.

"That gives me just enough time to have breakfast and do my make-up," said Lucy. "Did you upload the new web page?"

"Yeah, I was up till three, it looks really good, here I'll show you." Sara typed in the site address.

File Edit View Go Mailbox Help   **N**

Bookmarks   Location   http://www.lucylix.com

Young Model
Will Suck Your Cock
While Another Hot Chick
Videos The Action !!!

18 By entering this site you are confirming that you are over 18 years of age.

ENTER

Start

"Oh! Wow! Sara you're a genius. We're going to get loads of calls."

"And look Lucy, when you enter the site there's a photo of you sucking on a dildo. You'd better get ready, it's already eleven," said Sara. "Wear those new knickers you showed me last night."

Lucy went into the bedroom, tidied the bedclothes, and put on her panties and bra. Her pussy had fully recovered from the previous day. She placed some condoms and tissues on the bedside table, and lay on the bed.

There was a knock on the door.

"Come in, I've been waiting for you," purred Lucy.

Sara opened the door. "This is Jeremy, he's staying for half an hour. Have a good time."

"Hello Jeremy, I'm Lucy. What can I do for you?"

Jeremy seemed a bit shy, there was a silence.

"You can tell me Jeremy, I love sex, and I'm feeling very horny," Lucy said trying to encourage him.

"Well, I'd like to finger you, and then for you to give me hand relief so I come over your breasts."

"That sounds good to me Jeremy, I could do with a bit of relief myself. You had better take your clothes off."

Jeremy took off his clothes and put them on the chair. Lucy was surprised to see a good eight inches of flaccid cock hanging down between Jeremy's legs. He hadn't looked like he possessed such a monster when he had all his clothes on. Lucy started to take off her panties.

"Please leave your knickers on, I'll massage you through them."

"Okay Jeremy, what ever you say."

"Take off your bra though."

Lucy threw her bra on the floor. She sat cross-legged on the bed. Jeremy sat facing her, one leg either side so that his cock was just touching her panties. He told her to wrap her legs around him so that they could get closer. They were inches apart. Lucy stroked his cock, taking it in her hand, she rubbed the head up and down the front of her panties. He took her hand away, his cock standing straight, resting erect against Lucy's stomach. He found her clitoris and began to gently, slowly massage it in a circular motion through her panties.

"Ooh that feels good baby," Lucy purred.

He teased her, pressing slightly harder, but still with slow circular movements, using just one finger. Lucy gently touched his lips with hers, both staring into each others eyes. Lucy began to breath deeply, her breath going into his mouth. Her nipples were hard pushing into his chest. She could feel her wetness seeping through her panties as his finger circled slowly, teasing, rubbing her. Then she felt a second finger sliding further down, pushing into her cunt, running along the inside of her sex. Her panties were soaked through.

"Harder Jeremy, harder." Lucy pleaded. "Slide your hand in my knickers so you can go deeper."

But Jeremy ignored her pleas. Lucy looked down, his cock must have been ten inches erect. She again took the shaft in her hand, again he pushed it away.

"You will have to stop if you want me to last longer.

This feels so sexy, so intimate."

"Come now, come in your panties." Jeremy started to press harder and faster.

"Yes, yes harder, deeper, I'm coming . . ." Lucy kissed his lips as she came.

His fingers rubbed faster until Lucy could take no more and took his hand away.

"Now it's your turn Jeremy," said Lucy looking at his huge erection. Lucy grasped his cock, and immediately creamy cum spurted from the tip splattering her tits, covering them with semen. Lucy kept massaging as more and more cum ejaculated.

"Have you been saving that up for me? I've never seen so much."

"I haven't had sex for a few weeks, and I never masturbate."

"Why not?"

"It's Satan's pleasure." Jeremy replied.

"Don't be silly it's the most natural thing in the world, everybody does it all the time especially when they're single." Lucy said trying to put him at ease. What a weirdo she thought. There was a knock at the door.

"Oh dear, that means our time is up. I hope you enjoyed yourself. Don't leave it so long next time, you'll do yourself a mischief."

Jeremy put his clothes back on. Lucy washed the cum from her tits. The door opened. It was Sara.

"Is everything okay?" She asked.

"Oh yes, fine Sara, show Jeremy out."

"This way Jeremy, I hope you had a good time, come again." Sara closed the front door.

Lucy was laughing in the bedroom.

"I only just touched his prick, and it shot off like a fucking volcano, no wonder he has to come here, no woman would put up with that. And you should have seen the amount of spunk, it just never stopped coming out, I was covered. Although I have to say he gave me a good fingering."

"Do you fancy a trip to see that girl in the lingerie shop you were telling me about? We could have some fun," said Sara.

"Alright," replied Lucy. "We'll both wear something sexy. I know, we'll both wear tight jeans and tight T-shirts and no panties."

After dressing they were ready to go.

"Do I look okay Lucy?"

"You look gorgeous, she won't be able to take her eyes off your butt."

The girls went down to the lingerie shop, hoping that the assistant would be there.

Lucy looked through the rows of panties, while Sara checked out the assistant who was busy walking around the store checking that everything was in its proper place. She had a cute black bob hairdo, with big deep blue eyes and full red lips. Her tight cotton top accentuated her bosom, which her uplifting bra took full advantage of. Her skirt was also very short and tight, creasing where it covered her thighs. Her legs were bare and smooth. On her feet she wore high sandals. And of course she was wearing glasses, small rectangular black frames.

"She is delicious Lucy, let's go for it. We'll take some clothes into the changing room and then ask her to come in and give us a hand."

Lucy grabbed a handful of knickers, suspenders and basques, and off they went to the changing room.

"Nice and spacious, and with some cubicles for a bit of privacy," Sara remarked, "and lots of mirrors too."

"How are we going to get her to come in here?"

"Just let me get out of these jeans. I'll pretend I'm having trouble with the basque. Go and ask her to give us a hand will you Lucy."

Lucy went back out into the shop.

"Could you give my friend Sara a hand, she's trying to get into one of the basques."

"Yeah, sure, no problem," said the girl.

The name badge pinned to her chest read 'Yasmin'. They walked into the changing room to find Sara. She was naked except for the basque, and was pretending that she couldn't quite do up the clips at the back.

"Hi, I'm Sara, thanks for coming to my aid, I always have trouble getting into this sort of stuff. I think this is going to be fine, Lucy says she likes it, but I can't get these clips to meet properly."

Yasmin stood behind Sara and pulled the two sides of the basque tighter around her body to do up the clips.

"There, that's got it," said Yasmin as the final clip clicked into place. She smoothed her hands over the fabric of the basque to straighten it.

"What do you think, do I look sexy?" asked Sarah, looking directly at Yasmin.

"Yes you do, it fits you really well. You've got the body for it. But for the full effect you need stockings and the matching panties too. I'll get them for you if you want to try them all together."

"That would be brilliant. Let's go for the full effect. I'm feeling horny already."

Yasmin left the changing room.

"What d'you think Lucy?"

"Yeah, the way she was looking at you, I think she's interested."

Lucy kissed Sara lightly on the lips, and ran her fingers over her pussy.

"Well, you are horny Sara," Lucy said licking her fingers.

Yasmin came back carrying two small feminine boxes.

"Your man will love these," she said.

"Oh, I haven't got a man. Me and Lucy like to have fun."

Lucy held out her hand and Sara placed it on her breast. They both looked at Yasmin, watching for her response.

"Here, let me help you on with these," said Yasmin, taking the tiniest pair of panties from the box. "They are so sheer, just right for your neatly shaved pussy."

Sara's pussy was totally bare except for a triangle of soft hair just above her clitoris. Yasmin knelt down in front of Sara and held the panties so that she could step into them. Yasmin slid them up Sara's legs, making sure they fitted tightly to her curves. She lightly ran a finger over Sara's clitoris. Sara took Yasmin's hand and held it there, pressing Yasmin's fingers against her pussy. The panties were already wet through. Sara let go of Yasmin's hand but she didn't remove it, she slowly pushed her fingers into Sara's pussy, teasing her clit with her thumb. Then taking her hand away Yasmin pressed her mouth to Sara's cunt and began to suck her clit through the panties.

"That's so good, suck it Yasmin, ooh, suck me," pleaded Sara, opening her legs a little wider.

"Let's take these knickers down," Yasmin cooed. "I want to taste you."

Sara put her thighs together and Yasmin pulled the panties down, tossing them to one side. Then she parted Sara's pussy lips and pushed her tongue deep inside.

Lucy, who was still fully clothed, was sitting on one of the chairs playing with her nipples through her t-shirt. She could see the two girls' reflections in all the mirrors around the room, from every angle. She was feeling so hot and horny. She kicked off her shoes, and removed her jeans and t-shirt, walked over behind Yasmin, who was still licking out Sara, and slid a hand up her skirt. To Lucy's surprise she found that Yasmin wasn't wearing any panties. As her fingers found Yasmin's soaking pussy, Yasmin spread her legs apart sticking her arse out for Lucy's touch. Sara was now laying on her back with Yasmin's head between her legs. Yasmin was sucking and being fingered at the same time. Lucy lifted Yasmin's skirt up revealing her smooth soft buttocks, and pulling the cheeks apart buried her head between them, licking her pussy and making her moan with delight.

"Yasmin, suck me harder, push your tongue deeper, ooh yes, that's it," cried Sara.

Yasmin was looking up into Sara's eyes.

"Yes, yes, that's it, faster, faster, I'm coming. Don't stop! Yes, ooh, now, now, aah ooh." Sara flung her head back pushing her cunt into Yasmin's mouth as her orgasm peaked.

Now it was Yasmin's turn. Sara sat up, lifting Yasmin's head she kissed her on the lips, tasting her own juices. Lucy was still eating Yasmin's pussy, licking, sucking and teasing, her hands pulling her buttocks wide open, giving her mouth the deepest access. Sara pulled Yasmin's t-shirt over her head. Yasmin's breasts fell forward, they were big round and firm with pink luscious nipples, hard and begging to be sucked. Sara slid under Yasmin taking a nipple into her mouth, flicking it back and forth, gently biting it with her teeth.

"Fuck me, fuck me, make me come," shouted Yasmin.

Suddenly someone dropped a coat hanger.

Sara and Lucy looked up to see two schoolgirls, they must have been about fifteen years old, staring at them, their eyes were wide open, as if they were in a trance.

"Don't stop! I'm coming . . . fuck me, suck me!" cried Yasmin.

Sara kissed Yasmin and played with her nipples. Lucy, fingered Yasmin, both still watching the two schoolgirls.

Faster and faster Lucy fucked her. Yasmin's arse bucking with the ferocity of her orgasm, Yasmin let out an almighty scream as she climaxed and collapsed exhausted on the floor.

Opening her eyes, Yasmin suddenly caught sight of the two schoolgirls.

"How long have you two been watching us?" she demanded.

The two girls ran away giggling. Lucy and Sara started to giggle as well.

"We were really lucky nobody else walked in on us," said Yasmin, trying to get her breath back.

"You won't lose your job if those girls tell the owner will you?" asked Sara.

"Oh no, it's alright, I am the owner, well part-owner. I own fifty percent. My husband owns the other half. He lets me run this one as he's got lots of other business interests. As long as I make a profit, he lets me do as I like. I can't wait to tell him about this, he'll get so turned on. Knowing him, he'll probably want to join in, and have us all together. Perhaps another time."

Lucy and Sara looked at each other.

"Well, Sara wouldn't be up for it. She's saving it for Mr Right," Lucy said.

"What, Sara, you mean you've never had sex with a man?"

"Oh no, I want it to be special my first time."

"That's amazing," said Yasmin, gathering her clothes, "there aren't many girls these days of your age that haven't had sex."

"We'd better get dressed," said Sara, throwing Lucy her jeans, "you've got a punter tonight. One of your regulars"

"What do you girls do then?" asked Yasmin.

"I'm an escort. Sara takes my calls and makes my appointments for me."

"Do you have sex with your clients then?" asked Yasmin.

"If I want to," Lucy said nonchalantly, "like, if they're good looking and I fancy them, then I have sex." Lucy remembered all the sleazebags she'd had sex with.

When the girls were ready to go, Sara took out a card to give to Yasmin.

"Here's my address Yasmin, and my number. Give me a call won't you," Sara said kissing her on the lips.

Lucy and Sara headed for home.

"That card you gave to Yasmin has our website on the back Sara, do you think it will put her off calling you if she sees our site?"

"No, she seems pretty open-minded. Anyway, you're the one that does the blow-jobs, I just get the clients in!"

"Like a pimp you mean," laughed Lucy.

Lucy woke with a start.

"I think that there's someone at the door Sara, did you hear the buzzer?"

"What do you want me to do, you've got legs haven't

you? Sara snapped, burying her head under the covers.

"Alright, I'll go and see." Lucy climbed over Sara, pulling the blinds, letting the room flood with sunlight.

"Shit, Lucy, I wouldn't do that to you if you were still trying to sleep."

"Oh yes you would, and you have."

Lucy pressed the intercom.

"Hello."

"It's the postmen. I've got a parcel for you."

"I'll be right down."

Lucy opened the door.

"Here's your parcel Miss." The postman's jaw dropped, his eyes scanned Lucy's body, which had a lot of skin on show. Lucy looked down to see one breast poking out from beneath her dressing gown.

"Sorry to stare Miss, you just need to sign here."

Lucy took a long look at him, if he'd been a bit younger and a bit less ugly she'd have fucked him. She felt horny, she took another look. No she thought, I can wait. She signed and took the parcel.

"Thanks," she said and went back to the bedroom. "It's for you."

"For me!" Sara said excitedly. "I'll open it. I wonder what it is."

"Well the only way to find out is to *open it,*" Lucy replied sarcastically.

Sara quickly tore at the paper, and opened the box.

"It's from Yasmin, it's the basque and panties. What a lovely surprise! There's even some stockings. I'll put them on, after I've showered."

While Sara took a shower. Lucy fell asleep on the bed. She woke with a start, the telephone was ringing.

"Hello, Lucy and Sara's place," she said.

"Oh hello, is that the massage service?"

"Yes it is, you're speaking to the luscious Lucy."

"I was on the internet and I came across your website. You do a video service, where I can star in my own porn film?"

"Yes, a gorgeous young girl will video us while we have some fun."

"Could you tell me what the fee for this service is?"

"The cost is one hundred pounds for half an hour of anything goes sex, with a condom, but not anal, plus fifty pounds for the video service. You get to keep the video, you can watch yourself fucking me over and over."

"I've seen a photo of you on the web, you are lovely. I love brunettes with big tits. Could you tell me what the girl doing the filming looks like?"

"Certainly, Sara is really gorgeous, she has shoulder length blonde hair and big blue eyes. She's eighteen years old, with a firm body and pert little tits. Sara is every man's dream. But you can only look at Sara you can't touch."

"Book me for a whole hour. I like to take my time. Would two o'clock be good for you?"

"I'll just check the diary . . . yes that will be okay. What's your name?"

"Stephen."

" See you at two then Stephen."

"Oh just one other thing. Could you pretend that you're sweet and innocent, that it's the first time you've been with a man?"

"Yes of course, I love to role play, it will be a pleasure. I'll see you at two. Bye."

Sara appeared wearing the basque, panties, stockings and high-heels.

"What do you think Lucy? I feel really sexy in this. I can just imagine myself, legs parted, leaning against that wall being fucked from behind. If only Brad Pitt were here."

"I've told you before Sara, one cock's as good as the next. But I'm sure if Brad Pitt walked in right now, he'd have you up against the wall in no time. You can wear that this afternoon. We've got our first video session, and he's paying for one hour, two hundred and fifty pounds. I want it to go really well, he sounds quite rich, he wants me to pretend I'm a virgin."

"I'll check the camera and the lights, you can make the bed. Then I'll help you choose what to wear. Short white socks with that pleated navy blue mini skirt and a white blouse should do the trick. You'll look like a schoolgirl."

"Yeah, and my hair in pigtails. Oh and Sara, don't let me forget to put on some white panties. Come to think of it Sara don't wear that basque, you look too much like a high class hooker, wear something similar to me."

Sara put Lucy's hair in pigtails and they got dressed

up. They both looked like sixteen year olds.

"Come here Sara, you look so sweet and innocent." Lucy pulled Sara towards her and lifting her short skirt rubbed her fingers against the gusset of Sara's navy blue knickers. Then, easing the knicker elastic to one side, she slid two fingers along Sara's pussy lips.

"Ooh Lucy, stop, you'll get me all turned on."

"You're already nice and wet, it's just wearing these clothes, they're really making me horny as well." Lucy took her finger, from Sara's pussy and pushed it into Sara's mouth.

"Mmm, I taste nice and sweet," declared Sara sucking on Lucy's finger, "but then I am sweet sixteen."

"We are both sixteen for this next punter. He should be here any minute." Lucy looked out of the window to see if anyone was waiting at the front entrance. She could see a man crossing the road towards them, he was wearing a suit and had dark wavy hair. She also noticed a big black limousine, which seemed to have a chauffeur sitting in the drivers seat.

"Hey Sara come and look at this, if this is our guy, it looks like he's got his own limo and chauffeur. He must be rolling in it."

"Wow! Let's pull out all the stops, we'll be rich," exclaimed Sara. "And he's gorgeous, he looks like a film star!"

The intercom buzzed. Sara answered it.

"Hello, Lucy and Sara's place."

"Hello it's Stephen, I have a two o'clock appointment."

"Push the door and come straight up, it's apartment six, on the second floor."

Lucy opened the door to Stephen. He was in his mid-thirties, and even more good looking close-up. I'm going to enjoy this, she thought.

"Hello Stephen, I'm Lucy and this is my best friend Sara."

"Hi Stephen, come into the living room," said Sara. Would you like a coffee?"

"Yes that would be nice. Thank you."

"He's gorgeous!" Sara whispered to Lucy as she went into the kitchen. "I almost wish he was taking *my* virginity."

"Have a seat," said Lucy. "I'll move these books out of your way. We were doing our maths homework just before you arrived," she continued, getting straight into her role.

"Oh yes, what school do you go to?"

"The sixth form college in the town, the girls school at the top of the hill."

Lucy knelt in front of Stephen and rested her head on his thighs. She could make out the outline of his cock through his thin cotton dark tan trousers.

Sara returned with the coffee and placed it on the table next to Stephen.

"You always make such a mess Lucy," Sara said, deliberately turning her back to Stephen and bending over so that her panties were clearly visible, giving him a good view of her arse. She picked the books up off the floor.

Lucy noticed his cock growing, the tip of it was just one inch from her cheek straining against his trousers. Lucy moved herself towards it, so that she could feel its hardness.

"Stephen, you know I'm a virgin don't you? Well, I'd really like it if you were the first one," Lucy shyly said, looking up into his eyes.

"What do you mean the first one, the first one to what."

"You know the first one to touch me between my legs." Lucy pushed a hand into her crotch, showing Stephen where she meant. "I want *you* to take my virginity. I've never even touched a cock before. Let me touch yours, can I? *Please*."

Stephen unzipped his fly, and took out his penis.

"Can I see too?" said Sara excitedly.

Stephen's cock was standing erect. "Which one of you wants to touch it?" Stephen asked.

Lucy put her hand around the shaft, and caressed its length. "Ooh, isn't it big Sara?"

Sara placed her hand around its base and ran her fingers up to its tip. Lucy was surprised to see Sara joining in, she never usually touched the punters. It was obvious Sara was lusting after Stephen. "Yeah, it's so hard, big and beautiful," she said, "are you sure it's going to fit into your tight little pussy Lucy?"

"There's only one way to find out," said Stephen, "Let's go into the bedroom."

"I'll video you," said Sara, "I'll imagine it's me losing it to such a gorgeous hunk. You're so lucky Lucy."

Stephen followed the girls into the bedroom.

"You had better show me what to do Stephen," said Lucy, "I wouldn't want to disappoint you."

"Sit on the bed Lucy and pull your skirt up so I can see your panties. Yes that's right, just a bit higher. Now pull the gusset to one side so I can see your pussy. Yes that's lovely. Are you getting this Sara?"

"Yes, I'm filming everything. You look great Stephen."

Stephen was standing right in front of Lucy now.

"Unzip me Lucy and take my cock out."

Lucy did as he asked. She had his hardon in her hand gently rubbing it, watching it twitch inches from her mouth.

"Take it in your mouth Lucy."

Lucy opened her mouth, and slowly let the tip of his penis slide between her open moist lips, letting the small amount of lipstick she had on smear the end of his cock. Stephen immediately grabbed Lucy's head and pushed his whole length into her mouth, and began to slowly and rhythmically thrust backwards and forwards.

"Undo my belt Lucy."

The trousers dropped to the floor. Stephen wasn't wearing briefs.

"Now massage my arse with your hands Lucy."

Sara put the camera on the tripod, and with one hand started to finger herself, operating the camera with the other. Stephen pulled his cock out of Lucy's mouth. He looked at Sara, and she was looking straight at him.

"Now Lucy let's get those knickers off."

She lifted her bum up and he pulled them down.

"You have a lovely pussy Lucy, I bet it's nice and tight."

"You won't hurt me will you?" whispered Lucy, still playing her virgin role brilliantly.

He pushed a finger into her hot cunt. Lucy sighed. Sliding back further on to the bed she opened her legs wider.

"Take your blouse off, let me see your tits."

Lucy slowly unbuttoned her blouse. Shyly, she let it fall open to reveal her breasts. Stephen looked at Sara, she had both hands inside her panties.

"Would you like to join us Sara? You look like you want to." Stephen smiled.

"It's a very tempting offer . . . but no thanks."

"Why not?"

"Because I want my first time with a man to be something special."

"So you really are a virgin then?"

"Yes."

"I can make it special, I know you want to. I know you'd rather be in Lucy's place right now . . ."

"No."

"How much money would make it special then? What about five thousand pounds?" asked Stephen."

Sara looked at Lucy.

"Well what about ten then?" asked Stephen.

Lucy saw an opportunity.

"Sara's worth much more than that," Lucy said chancing her luck. "It would have to be twenty."

"Sara, will you fuck me for twenty?" asked Stephen.

Sara nodded.

"I'll just get my chauffeur to bring the money up." Stephen left the room to find his mobile.

"I can't believe this guy Sara. Surely he hasn't got twenty thousand pounds *in cash* in his car."

"Well, we'll soon find out."

"Are you sure you want to do this Sara?"

Before Sara could answer Stephen came back into the room.

"The money is on its way." Stephen announced triumphantly.

Lucy and Sara were both staring at Stephen's penis, which remarkably was still hard and erect.

"Once I get a hardon I rarely lose it until I've come."

The intercom buzzed. "Come up the door's open," Sara said pushing the button.

Lucy and Sara ran to the door to open it for the chauffeur, bearing what they hoped would be a big case of cash.

In the open doorway, in a blue suit with a peaked cap stood Yasmin.

"What are you doing here?" both girls said in unison.

"I've brought your money, twenty thousand pounds in cash."

"You're Stephen's chauffeur?" said Sara stunned.

"Only for today, I couldn't miss this could I? When I told him about the day you both came into the shop, he just had to meet you. I told him all about you, and when we had sex that night, it was wild. He just kept asking me to tell him over and over what the three of us had done, and when I told him you were a virgin Sara, he got *really* excited. Then we noticed your web site on the back of the card you gave me, and we went to look at it. You two really are very naughty aren't you!"

Yasmin walked to the table and putting the case down she opened the catches. The lid sprung up and inside were rows and rows of bundled-up notes.

"Wow!" Lucy cried, "I've never seen so much money."

Sara looked in the case.

"Come on then Sara," said Stephen, "if you want it you've got to earn it first."

Sara turned round smiling. "Are you going to video this for posterity Lucy?"

"Of course! I wouldn't miss this for the world. Come on Yasmin you can help me."

Stephen sat on the bed.

"Come here Sara, I'm going to take your clothes off."

Sara stood in front of him. Stephen lifted her skirt and ran his hands over her navy blue knickers, down between her legs pushing the cotton into the contours of her virgin pussy. Sara opened her legs a little wider.

"Turn around Sara."

He pulled the back of her panties down. He kissed her cheeks pushing his face between them, he licked her, searching her arse with his tongue. Then he pulled her knickers back up. Turning her, he unbuttoned her blouse. Her young breasts were level with his lips, her nipples

JUST PRESS PLAY

were hard. He pulled her towards him and teased them with his tongue, flicking them back and forth. Her blouse was on the floor now, her blonde hair covered her face as her head tossed gently from side to side. Stephen's hands were inside her panties, one in the crack of her arse the other sliding along her pussy lips up to her clitoris. She was soaking wet. Two fingers found her clit and he began to gently massage, with the other hand he pulled her knickers down. Sara stepped out of them. Then Stephen pulled down the zip at the back of the skirt, it fell to the floor. All Sara was wearing now were high sandals and short white socks. Stephen fell back on to the bed pulling Sara down on top of him. His hard cock touched her pussy lips but Stephen was careful not to let it slide in.

"I want it inside me." Sara begged, feeling it so close.

"First I'm going to eat your virgin pussy."

Stephen turned her on to her back, and slid down her belly to her cunt. Sara's thighs were already parted. Her pussy was glistening with sex juice. Stephen licked her clitoris making her writhe with pleasure. She clamped her legs tightly around his back pulling him closer.

"Oh yes! I want you inside me. Please . . . please," she cried. "Fuck me!"

Stephen lifted his head. He took his cock in his hand, and rubbed the tip around Sara's cunt. Slowly teasing the lips apart. Then gently he pushed into her.

"Oooh yes, Sara purred. "Push it right in . . . yes . . . yes! It hurts so good". Her pussy was so tight.

Lucy was filming everything. Every thrust, every expression. Recording every sigh, every moan. Yasmin had taken her clothes off. She was leaning, with her back against the wall fingering her pussy, watching the action. Stephen was on top, with his hands under Sara's bottom, his fingers were teasing her arse as he thrust deeply into her.

"Your cunt's so fucking tight, it's beautiful." Stephen withdrew his cock. He twisted Sara around so that he could take her from behind, she was on all fours with her legs spread and her arse in the air. Sara reached between her legs, took hold of his penis and guided it back into her pussy.

"Ooh, that feels so good. Deeper, fuck me *deeper*!" Sara pleaded, spreading her legs apart further so her cunt was wide open.

Stephen had both hands on her hips pulling her towards him as he pumped into her.

"Lucy, film Yasmin I think she's going to come," said Stephen.

Lucy quickly turned the camera on Yasmin. She was finger fucking herself, sitting on the floor, her back against the wall. Lucy zoomed in on her pussy. Three fingers were inside, her thumb rubbed her clit. Faster and faster she fucked herself, her left hand frantically pulling painfully at her hard nipples. Lucy was capturing it all. Then Yasmin began to orgasm, her back arched, her legs parted.

"Yes . . . yes," she cried. "I'm coming. Oooh yes, yes."

She squeezed her thighs tightly together, and rolled

over on to her side as her orgasm subsided. Lucy turned the camera back on Sara and Stephen. They were fucking in the missionary position, Stephen's hands were under Sara's bum, lifting her up to meet his thrusts, his small muscular arse setting the rhythm. Their lips were pressed together, kissing each other deeply. Sara began to moan and Stephen's thrusts became faster. Lucy could see his big cock sliding in and out of Sara's young pussy.

"Oh Stephen I'm coming," Sara cried. "Harder . . . harder! Fuck me, fuck me."

"Yes, yes . . ." shouted Stephen, his thrusts becoming slower but more forceful. He climaxed shooting his hot cum into her cunt.

Sara was still in the throws of her own orgasm. Her slender fingers frantically rubbed her clit as she came again and again, biting her bottom lip as wave after wave of raw pleasure surged through her body.

Lucy had never seen Sara orgasm so powerfully before. Stephen was spent, he lay to one side, to be replaced by Yasmin's eager tongue, licking and sucking Sara's wet pussy, tasting its sweetness. Sara, sexually exhausted, relaxed on the bed. Yasmin lay between her legs licking her lips.

"Wow, that was some hot, hot sex," said Lucy putting the camera back on its tripod. "I can't wait to see it."

"Yeah," said Yasmin, "you'll both have to come to our house to see it won't they Stephen?"

"Of course, we can do this again, and watch the movie." Stephen looked like he was the cat that got the cream.

"We had better get going Stephen, remember we've got tickets for the theatre tonight."

"Shit, I didn't realise it was that late."

Yasmin and Stephen quickly dressed and left.

Lucy brought the case into the bedroom and put it on the bed.

"We're rich!" said Lucy.

Sara sat up and looked at the cash. Taking a handful she tossed it in the air.

Watching it fall all around her she cried, "Wow! Twenty thousand pounds, and I was so fucking horny I was going to fuck him anyway."

Bettina writes,

As in my first book, I've left these pages free in case you want to write down your own secret desire. Maybe your wish will come true . . .

My Secret Desire

MY SECRET DESIRE

Dear Reader,

I hope you have enjoyed my second collection of stories.

If you would like to be on my mailing list, please return the slip at the back of this book. You will be the first to know about new books, limited editions, and special offers of sexy items.

I love receiving your letters, just send them c/o Collective Publishing. They always forward them on to me, wherever I am.

Till next time . . .
Lots of love,

Bettina
xxx

credits . . .

TEACHER'S PETS .... Belladonna

SISTERS IN SIN .... Tony Leather

BACK SEAT BITCHES .... Rebecca Ambrose

SPANKING .... Charles Davenant

RIDING A JAGUAR .... Debbie Smith

COMING CLEAN .... Maria Lyonesse

All other stories told to, and written down by
Bettina Varese and Candy Lace.

**COLLECTIVE
PUBLISHING**

sugar-coated babies
on a trashed-out trip to nowhere

destination
pulp

*PLEASE SEND ME INFORMATION
ABOUT NEW PUBLICATIONS
LIMITED EDITIONS
SPECIAL OFFERS*

NAME ....

ADDRESS ....

....

....

....

POSTCODE ....

COUNTRY ....

e-mail:

Please return this slip to:

Bettina Varese
c/o COLLECTIVE PUBLISHING
P. O. BOX 10
SUNBURY ON THAMES
TW16 7YG
ENGLAND U.K.

Please see reverse for book ordering details

What they said about

'Erotica 1: Bettina's Tales'

" a collection of sexy tales from the lovely Bettina . . . . . . fast, cheap thrills" FORUM

" strong stuff . . ." DESIRE MAGAZINE

To order please fill in this form:

Please send me
Erotica 1: Bettina's Tales ☐
ISBN 0 9535290 0 2

NAME ....

ADDRESS ....

....

....

POSTCODE ....

COUNTRY ....

I enclose a cheque/postal order, made payable to **The Collective**, for £4.99 plus postage (UK add £1.00/ overseas add £2.00)

Please send your order to:
COLLECTIVE PUBLISHING
P. O. BOX 10, SUNBURY ON THAMES
TW16 7YG, ENGLAND U.K.